S0-BHT-464

Window of Hope

Katherine,

by

Thanks for all you do.
Stay Positive ! Millie

Millie Curtis

Millie Curtis

Avid Readers Publishing Group
Lakewood, California

This is a work of fiction. The opinions expressed in this manuscript are those of the author and do not represent the thoughts or opinions of the publisher. The author warrants and represents that she has the legal right to publish or owns all material in this book. If you find a discrepancy, contact the publisher at www.avidreaderspg.com.

Window of Hope

All Rights Reserved

Copyright © 2014 Millie Curtis

This book may not be transmitted, reproduced, or stored in part or in whole by any means without the express written consent of the publisher except for brief quotations in articles and reviews.

Avid Readers Publishing Group

http://www.avidreaderspg.com

ISBN-13: 978-1-61286-232-3

Printed in the United States

This book is dedicated to the memory of Thomas R. Wilson: my brother, my hero, and my proud World War II member of the United States Marine Corps.

He never met a stranger nor saw a tree he didn't love.

ACKNOWLEDGEMENTS

When a novel is completed there are many to thank for their assistance. This book is no exception. Therefore, I say thank you to the following:

Tara Bell, Ginny Fite and Karen Robbins: my helpful writing group who are all published authors and whose critique I welcome.

Elizabeth Blye: new mother and lovely daughter who has rescued me from too many computer glitches. She is also the talented photographer and creator of the photos on the front and back covers.

Rebecca Moran: another lovely daughter who carted around the three young ladies who posed for the pictures on the book cover.

Jordann Jenkins, Anica Moran, Anna Sule: the three young ladies who graciously consented to become models for a day. I also thank their moms for allowing the girls to be the subjects of photography for this novel.

Fred Curtis, Jean Malucci, Amy Nishimoto and Catherine Owens: they performed the laborious job of proofreading.

Eric Patterson with Avid Readers Publishing Group: the one who put it all together.

And you, dear readers, thank you for your kind words and encouragement to keep writing.

Chapter 1

Three close friends stood together on the platform of Union Station in Washington, D.C. as their husbands boarded the train that was taking them off to war.

Dressed in fashionable coats, hats and boots of 1917, the three young women had taken special care to look their best. They were as different in appearance and temperament as night is to day, but those qualities, along with life's circumstances, tightened their bond.

Crowds consisting of aged grandparents to babes in their mothers' arms pushed and shoved their way to the edge of the platform to get one last glimpse or one last touch of a loved one. A mixture of sentiments from tears to hurrahs was heard and resounded in the hollow walls of the large station.

The three women shed no tears. They stood erect, held miniature USA flags, and watched their men prepare to go off to God knows what, pretending they agreed it was the patriotic thing to do.

The husbands, too, showed a stoic side as they found seats in the railcar and waved to their young wives while the train chugged out of the station.

With every chug of the engine the women felt a tug on their hearts.

They could blame President Wilson. He was the one who had declared war.

No, the blame went to the power-hungry Germans. They were the rightful ones to bear the bitter resentment.

Perhaps it was the duty of the men to defend their country and leave the women to carry on at home. But, war has a way of changing lives; a fact the three women knew full well.

**

Catherine Burke, twenty-six, and a milliner by trade, turned to address the other two. "I stopped short of pleading with Patrick not to go. After all, he just finished his medical training and was looking for a place to open his office. It doesn't seem fair."

"It's not fair to any of us," replied her friend, Carolyn. "I always told Asa I was not fond of his Army career."

Elizabeth Caldwell, the youngest at twenty-one, had only been married to her tall, handsome Andrew for five months, hardly enough time for newlyweds to get to know each other. "Carolyn, our husbands are in the Army. They had to follow orders. Patrick had a choice and he chose to help his fellow man."

Carolyn Thomas, twenty-four and a nurse by profession, was not in a compassionate mood. She pulled her wool shawl tighter around her shoulders and glowered at the young woman with blond hair peeking from under her cloche hat. "Don't be so understanding. I'm mad!" Her dark eyes flashed with displeasure.

"Carolyn, we're all upset! Don't take your discontent out on Elizabeth," snapped Catherine.

The remark hit home and Carolyn offered a half-hearted apology, "I'm sorry."

Elizabeth was not to be placated. "I'm the one who should be most upset. At least you have a comfortable house on the base. I have to live with my parents!"

Carolyn opened her mouth to shoot another dart before she was cut off by Catherine's caustic censure.

"Both of you! Stop that bickering! You sound like spoiled children." Her voice softened, "Look, we have each other, and we are going to need each other. Who knows when our husbands will return, in what shape they will be, or even if they will come home."

The words brought Carolyn to attention. "Good heavens, Catherine!"

Elizabeth dabbed her eyes with a handkerchief. "She's right, Carolyn. We don't know what the future will bring."

Catherine adjusted the scarf she wore inside her fur jacket. "We need to be prepared for any outcome, run our lives as though we were widows."

Upon hearing that, Elizabeth boohooed all the tears she'd held in check.

Carolyn put a sympathetic arm around her friend's shoulders. "For heaven's sake. Now look what you've done, Catherine."

There was a heavy sigh. "Perhaps I should have voiced it differently. This whole day is falling apart. Let's not stand here looking glum, Mattie's probably up to her ears with your two little ones."

Elizabeth dried her eyes and sniffed her response, "I'm half upset with myself. It took all my willpower, but I refused to cry in front of Andrew. I guess those tears were waiting to break through."

"Cry all you want," said a vexed Catherine. "I'm going to hail a taxi to take us over to my house to relieve my maid." She turned and strode out of the station.

Carolyn tucked a strand of long dark hair back under her blue felt fedora. "Ooh, Catherine's in a snit. That's unlike her. We'd better hustle."

Elizabeth pulled on leather gloves as they prepared to leave. "We should reward Mattie for watching the children."

"I suggested that to Catherine and she said Mattie would be offended because she offered out of the goodness of her heart."

Elizabeth took a delicate swipe at her nose with a flowered handkerchief before putting it back into her coat pocket. "I don't care. A little some-thing isn't going to bruise Mattie's pride." She hurried back to buy a candy bar from a vendor in the station.

The taxi pulled to the street curb as Carolyn hurried to meet the disgruntled Catherine.

"Where's Elizabeth? The hackie will charge us more if he has to wait."

Carolyn was about to explain Elizabeth's absence when she spied her, with coat and skirt flapping, coming on the run.

One by one they stepped up onto the running board of the Model T taxi and squeezed into the back seat.

Each was lost in her own thoughts. The only sounds were the rattle of the car and the tinny sound of the engine as the noisy Ford made its way down M Street toward the Burke house in Georgetown.

**

Catherine and Carolyn had become like sisters when Catherine owned a millinery shop in Berryville, Virginia, and Carolyn was the office nurse for Dr. Hawthorne, the physician in town.

When Carolyn met and married Asa Thomas, a captain in the U.S. Cavalry, and moved to Washington, D.C., her absence left a void in Catherine's life until the well-to-do Patrick Burke came to town for a wedding.

After a short courtship, Catherine gave up her independent way of life for marriage and moved to Patrick's house in Georgetown, but not before she had to solve the dilemma of what to do with the hat shop.

That problem was answered when Elizabeth's parents bought the millinery in Berryville to give their daughter a new start in life.

It was there in Clarke County that Elizabeth met Captain Andrew Caldwell of Red Gate Farm. A whirlwind romance led to marriage, much to her parents' approval and sighs of relief.

As these six lives intertwined: Catherine and Patrick, Carolyn and Asa, Elizabeth and Andrew, the three couples became close-knit.

Chapter 2

The cab pulled in front of a two-story, red brick house setting back from the street.

Mattie, Catherine's colored maid, and a giant of a woman, stepped out onto the porch as the young ladies walked up the brick walk.

She closed the door behind her and cautioned them with a finger to her full lips. "The two little ones be down for a nap upstairs in the bedrooms. It won't do to wake 'em up or they'll be cross as bears. There's tea and sandwiches ready in the kitchen."

Catherine offered a weak smile. "Thank you, Mattie. It is just what we need."

Before opening the door, the maid gave a concerned look. "You gots Mistah' Patrick and the other men off?"

"As much as we hated to see them go, we put on a united front."

Mattie shook her head, opened the door and they followed her down the hallway into the kitchen. They draped their outerwear over the backs of straight chairs and put their hats on a shelf near the rear door before taking seats at the small round oak table.

"Were Annie and Matthew any trouble?" asked Carolyn.

Mattie was fixing tea. Although she was a large woman, she had a certain style and easy grace that stated the kitchen was her domain. "No ma'am. But, I was hard-put to keep up with 'em.'"

"Oh, how well I know. Matthew keeps me on my toes," said Elizabeth.

Carolyn's response was meant to sound weary, but there was a glimmer of pride in her words, "Now that Annie has started walking, she explores everything. It's like she's found the world full of wonder."

"I would say she takes after her mother in that respect," came Catherine's tongue-in-cheek reply.

Elizabeth allowed a wide grin to spread across her pretty face.

Carolyn flipped her hair back over her shoulder. "I'm glad you're in a better mood, my dear Catherine. Jest if you will, but there is much to explore in this world of ours."

Mattie brought the tea to the table and poured it into their china cups. She lifted a linen tea towel from a silver platter containing finger sandwiches on one side and delicate cookies on the other.

"Mattie, how could you possibly have prepared this delicious looking lunch with the children under foot?" asked Elizabeth.

"I done closed that door so's they couldn't git out of this kitchen an' gave 'em pots and wooden spoons to play with. Then I left those cupboard doors open so's they could crawl in an' out."

"No wonder they were tired," Carolyn enjoined as she reached for a sandwich filled with ham salad.

Mattie went back to her duties around the stove. The three young women sipped their tea.

Between nibbles of her sandwich, Carolyn announced, "I think I'm going to get my hair bobbed."

Catherine scowled. "Why would you want to do that? Would Asa approve?"

"I've heard it's all the rage," Elizabeth offered. "We've shortened our skirts, and our hat brims for this war, why not shorten our hair?"

"Elizabeth, I'm sure Andrew does not want you to cut off that long blond hair," cautioned Catherine.

Carolyn made a face at her friend. "You said we should start living as widows, so, if we do, it doesn't matter what our husbands think."

"That isn't exactly what I meant."

Carolyn's enthusiasm was contagious bringing Elizabeth to life. "Let's do it! Our men will be gone for at least six months. That will give time for our hair to grow back."

"Where did six months come from?" asked Catherine.

"From Andrew," said Elizabeth. "Andrew said the American Expeditionary Forces are to be in Europe for six months."

"General Pershing has sent Asa and Andrew to set up training camps in France. They will be away from the front lines," informed Carolyn.

"I worry about Patrick," Catherine lamented. "He is going to be doctoring in one of those field hospitals, and they are near the front lines."

Carolyn touched her shoulder. "It's unlike you to be a worry-wart. I guess that's why you've been a bit testy."

A faint smile appeared on Catherine's pleasant face. If Carolyn only knew.

Elizabeth rose from her chair. "I'm going up and check on the children. How long have they been napping, Mattie?"

"I 'spect a bit over an hour," she answered while clearing away the dishes.

Elizabeth left the kitchen.

After she was gone, Carolyn lowered her voice almost to a whisper. "There is something besides Patrick troubling you."

"What do you mean?"

"I know you too well. It's not like you to be short with people, especially with me and Elizabeth."

The clamor from above broke into the moment and announced the two little ones were up.

"I would prefer to stay and drag it out of you, but I'll go up and help Elizabeth. This conversation isn't finished," said a reluctant Carolyn.

When she reached the upper floor, she found the delicate Elizabeth was no match for the two toddlers. They were struggling to break away when Carolyn arrived on the scene.

"I'm glad to see you. I'm not strong enough to handle both of them."

Carolyn picked up her daughter, Ann Catherine. The relieved fourteen-month old threw her arms around her mother's neck as though never to let her go.

Elizabeth leaned over and picked up a crib blanket and stuffed teddy bear from the bed while she held the squirming Matthew. He grabbed for the blanket as though it was a long lost friend. By the time the fastidious Elizabeth smoothed the bed covers and checked the room, to be sure nothing was out of place, Carolyn had descended the stairs.

In the kitchen, the children must have remembered the pots and spoons because they started whining and pushing, trying to get out of their mothers' arms.

Oblivious to the mothers and without a word, Mattie walked over and plucked them, one by one, under each solid arm.

"I done got somethin' special fer you little ones. I don' wanna' hear no cryin' or blubberin'." With authority, she sat each on a high stool pulled up to the table. They stopped fussing and looked at her wide-eyed.

"I done made custard to sweeten 'em up," she announced.

Carolyn grabbed a tea towel and tied it around Annie's neck. "They're going to make a mess."

Elizabeth was to the point. "I'll feed Matthew. I don't want him looking like an urchin when I take him home."

"Yessum," agreed Mattie, who turned and mumbled to herself, loud enough for all to hear, "messin's good fer little ones."

"Mattie's right, Elizabeth," said Carolyn. "You should let Matthew feed himself."

"If I let him go at it, he'll have it in his hair and all over me. No thank you. I'll feed him."

Carolyn shrugged her shoulders, and Mattie placed the custard on the table.

"That looks good. Did you make any more?" Catherine asked. "I'd like to have a dish."

"I made one of them custard pies."

Elizabeth turned quickly from attending to Matthew. The mention of custard pie made her blue eyes light up. "You did?"

"I say we all have a piece," offered Catherine.

Elizabeth had a change of heart. "On second thought, Carolyn, pull one of those diapers out of my bag. I can't turn down a piece of custard pie!"

The dessert seemed to sweeten everyone's disposition. Custard faces, fingers and hands were cleaned without a complaint from child or mother.

They were getting the children dressed to leave when Elizabeth remembered the Hershey candy bar she'd bought for Mattie. Away from Catherine's view, she pulled it from her tote bag and slid it into the maid's apron pocket. "Thanks, Mattie," she whispered into the maid's ear.

Mattie never uttered a sound nor cracked a smile, but she did pat her apron pocket.

Both Elizabeth and Carolyn hugged Catherine, who in turn hugged them and kissed the cheeks of the little ones.

She stood on the porch and watched, with a wistful eye, as her friends carried their cherished offspring down the brick walk. Ann Catherine was her Godchild. The dark-eyed child with coal black hair held a special place in her heart.

She smiled as Elizabeth put Matthew down after they left the porch steps. He was two months older than Ann Catherine but a head taller and becoming a struggle for Elizabeth to carry.

"He's going to be taller than you one of these days, Elizabeth," she called.

They all turned and waved.

Her friends could be unhappy that their husbands were gone, but they had their children. Catherine Burke had no one. She knew the raw, gnawing, feeling of loneliness and was loathe to face it again. And then there was the other problem.

**

Carolyn Thomas sat on the trolley heading for the army base with Annie standing on her lap. Little Ann Catherine was contented looking out the window, watching the wonder of Washington, D.C. pass by: tall buildings, buggies, taxies, men in top hats, beggars.

Carolyn, as parents often do, thought her little one was the cutest and brightest child she had ever seen. Yet, there were times when she wished

Annie had not arrived so soon in her marriage. She and Asa had not been married quite a year when their little one was born.

Motherhood held her back from the freedom to come and go. She wanted to get more nursing experience and more involved in the Suffragette movement. What better place to fight for one's right than in the nation's capitol?

Carolyn had met Asa when she was caring for Virginia Caldwell at Red Gate Farm, a large estate in Virginia. He was a captain in the U.S. Calvary and had come on a visit with his good friend, Andrew Caldwell. Asa had swept her off her feet. Perhaps it was more truthful to say that she had swept him off his feet.

At first, she was unsure about her feelings toward him. But, when he was close to death after being knifed trying to stop a brawl outside Union Station, she knew her life wouldn't be complete without her gallant Asa. So, even though she was not fond of army life, they married after a short courtship.

Ann Catherine had been a difficult birth. Asa was in England on an army assignment at the time. Carolyn was staying in Berryville, Virginia, with Catherine, who owned a millinery. They grew to be more like sisters than friends as Catherine became her strong support throughout the ordeal.

Her musings stopped when Annie grew tired of looking out the window and settled onto her mother's lap. Carolyn smiled at her, kissed her cheek and pulled her close. Politics would have to wait.

As she sat quietly holding her little daughter, her mind returned to the painful separation she had experienced a few short hours ago.

What if Asa didn't return from this awful war? What if her precious Annie was left without a father? What if she was left without a husband? What if? What if? She pushed the thoughts to the back of her mind.

**

Two blocks from her parents' home in Alexandria, Virginia, across the Potomac River from Washington, D.C., Elizabeth Caldwell walked slowly so Matthew could toddle along beside her. He was getting too heavy for her to carry any distance.

She knew her parents would be home. They were always home. With Andrew gone, there would be no one to buffer the friction between mother and daughter.

It had always been that way. Her grand-mother had been the intervener when Elizabeth was young. When she died, Elizabeth was sent to finishing school, which may have been a blessing as she only had to deal with her mother on holidays.

This situation of living with her parents was supposed to be a temporary fix until Andrew could get base housing. Here it was going into the sixth month and no house had become available.

Although she was not a deeply religious person, Elizabeth believed Andrew to be God-sent.

He had adopted Matthew as his own and had given him his name, although that wasn't well-received by his Virginia family. What man would accept an illegitimate child and the tainted mother unless he was a loving and forgiving person?

It had been heart-wrenching to watch him ride away on the train. At the thought, Elizabeth swallowed the lump in her throat and squeezed her eyes shut.

Matthew had found a stick and was hitting every tree and bush as they walked along the sidewalk.

They arrived at the house when the stick broke on the slat of an iron picket fence and he started howling.

Elizabeth picked him up. "Hush, Matthew. Mommy will find you another stick."

Before she could calm him, Gertrude Fairchilds appeared on the porch.

"Elizabeth, what is that racket? Get the child in here before he disturbs the neighbors."

"I'm sorry, Mother. He was playing with a stick and it broke and…"

"You are just going to have to teach him that bawling is not acceptable behavior."

Elizabeth patted her son's back to soothe him. "Mother, at his age, do you really think he would understand?"

"Nevertheless, children should be made to behave. Opal has dinner ready." She turned on her heel and tromped into the house.

Perhaps the mother was getting as tired of the daughter living there as the daughter was tired of being ordered about. Especially, when it came to the care of her child.

Elizabeth's father surprised her as he came walking around the side of the house.

He patted Matthew's back. The child had settled down to a whimper.

"Rough day, Lizzy?

She nodded.

"Get Andrew off okay?"

She nodded again.

"Here. Let me take this little fellow and we'll get some dinner. We're all going to have some lonesome days before Andrew gets back."

Dispirited, Elizabeth followed her father into the house.

Something had to change!

Chapter 3

Two weeks later, Catherine picked up the telephone. "Hello."

"Catherine, its Carolyn." She sounded anxious.

"Is everything all right?"

"No, it isn't. I am so bored and missing Asa so much, I can't stand it. Have you heard from Patrick?"

"Not a word."

Anxiety turned to annoyance. "You would think they would be settled by now and would write a note."

"I'm sure they will let us know where they are as soon as they can. It isn't like they went down the block."

"You're right. I guess I'm being a ninny. Sometimes I wonder if I'm losing my mind. What would you say if I told you that I'm thinking about joining the Army Nurse Corps?"

There was hesitation before Catherine answered, "I would say you aren't losing your mind, you've already lost it."

"I have been giving this idea a lot of thought."

"You have a daughter, Carolyn. Have you thought of her?"

"Of course I have. Here's my plan. You can go with me and take care of Annie while I work in the hospital."

"Hold on one minute. What hospital? Where?"

"I don't know. England? France? One of the field hospitals, maybe."

"Now you are talking crazy. There's a war going on over there. People are getting killed. I think I should come over to your place."

Carolyn nixed that suggestion. "No, I'll come over to see you. I've got to get out of this house."

"Can you come this afternoon?"

"Perfect," said Carolyn. "I'll catch the noon trolley. Do you want me to bring a couple of sandwiches?"

"I'll have Mattie fix us lunch and then we can talk."

Carolyn's heavy sigh was heard over the phone. "Good. Annie and I will be there."

Feeling dazed, Catherine hung up the receiver.

**

Carolyn arrived on Catherine's doorstep shortly after noon with Ann Catherine in her arms.

Mattie opened the door. "Miz' Carolyn, it's good to see you." She lifted Annie from her mother's arms. "Look at you, chile' I done think you growed. Let Miz' Mattie take off your bonnet."

Carolyn had slipped off her coat and was unpinning her hat when she heard Catherine call,

19

"I'll be right there." She came hurrying down the stairs. "You made a fast trip."

"We took the first trolley coming this way."

Mattie was still holding Annie, who had a bear hug around her neck. "Miz' Carolyn, how 'bout I take Annie up to rock in the big rockin' chair upstairs? I done got lunch on the table, an' you and Miz' Catherine can have a nice talk."

"Is that all right with you, Catherine?" asked Carolyn.

"It's a splendid idea. Thank you for thinking of it, Mattie."

"I fed Annie lunch before we left the house so she might fall asleep."

Mattie patted the little one's dark hair. "Likely we both might start dozin'. That there chair's like magic. We be fine, Miz' Carolyn." Off she went up the stairs with Annie in her arms.

Catherine gave Carolyn a sisterly hug. "I'm glad you're here. Mattie loves the little ones. It's sad she never had any of her own."

They started for the kitchen.

"How old is she?" asked Carolyn.

"I don't know. I never asked her. If you'll pour the tea, I'll dish up the soup."

They sat at the small round oak table, where Mattie had left finger sandwiches and scones.

"I wish we'd get some word from the men," said Carolyn.

"Have you talked with Elizabeth? Perhaps she's heard from Andrew."

"I phoned her the other day. She's not received word, either. Her mother is driving her nutsy-cuckoo."

"That makes two of you. When you're both committed, I'll be kept busy visiting in the asylum."

Carolyn gave a disgusted look. "That isn't funny."

"I'm sorry. Tell me about this whim of yours."

"It isn't a whim. I have been doing my research. If I join the Army Nurse Corps, they will send me to either England or France. You can go with me and take care of Annie so I won't have to be away from her. We can find a place where Asa and Patrick can come to when they have some time."

"And they all lived happily ever after." Catherine shook her head. "It is a war, Carolyn. A real war is not a nice little fairy tale. If you're intent on helping, you can do it right here. Women are driving buses and taxies and working in the factories. If all the nurses go running off to Europe, who's going to be left here to run the hospitals?"

"Nurses are needed over there."

"They're needed over here."

"Catherine, where is your sense of adventure?"

Removing the tea cozy and checking to be sure the tea was still hot, Catherine poured it into their cups.

21

"My sense of adventure does not include going to Europe when there's a war raging."

"It's not as though we are going to be in the thick of things."

"I am not going. Do you recall saying that you knew there was something on my mind?"

"Of course."

"Then listen carefully. What's on my mind is that I think I am expecting a baby, and I'm…"

"A baby!" Carolyn's mouth was agape. "No wonder you were touchy. I knew it had to be something besides the fact Patrick was leaving. Did you tell him?"

"Of course not."

"Perhaps you should have. He wouldn't have gone."

Catherine inclined her head toward her friend. "And that wouldn't have been fair to him."

"As fair as leaving you to face this by yourself."

"What's done is done and I'm not going to second-guess it. My concern is this. If there is a baby on the way, I'm not sure the process is going as well as it is supposed to."

"Have you seen a doctor?"

"No. I don't know who to see. I thought you might have some nursing advice in that department."

Carolyn listened to Catherine's concerns and brightened when an idea popped into her head. "Why don't you go to Berryville and see Dr. Hawthorne? He's the best baby doctor around."

"I know he is, but he's seventy miles away. Where would I stay?"

"Elizabeth says the hat shop you sold her still hasn't had a buyer. We could stay upstairs in your old apartment."

Catherine smiled. "Now it's we? I don't know. I live here now. I should see a doctor nearby. Besides, that would be an imposition on Elizabeth. And, I sold the shop to her parents."

Carolyn was finishing a scone. "Elizabeth owns it. They signed it over to her after she married Andrew."

Catherine gave a knowing look. "Yes, Elizabeth told me. She also said she wished it would sell so she didn't have to worry about it sitting idle."

"Let's go, Catherine. You left most of the furniture. It'll do us both good to get a change of scenery," Carolyn encouraged. "We'll go just for a visit and Dr. Hawthorne can tell you if he suspects there will be problems."

Catherine gave a wry smile. "You're just antsy to go someplace."

"I won't say that isn't part of it. Look how he pulled me through Annie's birth. If I hadn't had him, either she or I or both might not be here. Let's call Elizabeth. Maybe she'll go with us."

Catherine put up her hands. "Whoa. I haven't agreed to anything."

"But you will. I'm going to call Elizabeth right now."

23

Catherine didn't protest. She cleared away the dishes as Carolyn went to the living room to pick up the phone. She smiled to herself, at least her friend was off the ridiculous idea of joining the Army Nurse Corps.

Carolyn rushed back into the kitchen. "She's all for it! Elizabeth says the hat shop is still unoccupied and it would be good for her to check on it."

"I suppose you told her I was expecting a child."

"Of course not. That's up to you. I told her you needed to go see Dr. Hawthorne, which is the truth because you are unsure."

Catherine sat resting her elbows on the table, her hands under her chin. "Naturally, she didn't put two and two together."

"She didn't ask any questions. Women can have other problems besides having babies."

Carolyn stood behind Catherine and put her arms around her neck pressing their cheeks together. "Come on. Let's be happy. This will be a little adventure to get our minds off the men being gone."

Catherine mulled over the possibility. "I've already closed up the hat shop I have here because there won't be a lot of buying now that we are into the war. Mattie can keep an eye on the house, so I guess I have no excuse. How long will we be gone?"

Carolyn stood up and went back to the chair she had vacated. "I'd like to stay for a week...or two. I want to take Annie to visit my parents for a couple of days. They've never seen her."

"You should. Elizabeth will have an obligation to see Andrew's parents at Red Gate Farm no doubt, and I know she and I will want to visit Mary Lee. Maybe I can get Irene Butler to make some expanding clothes." She laughed. "Yes, I think a trip back will be good for all of us."

The enthused Carolyn popped up from her seat. "I can't wait to see Lavinia Talley's face. The busybody will be fluttering around like a butterfly. I'll make all the arrangements. We can leave on Monday. That will give us four days to get ready. Do you think Mattie will pack us a lunch to eat on the train?"

Then a quick after-thought, "You do feel up to it, Catherine?

"I do. Perhaps it's what we all need. I know Mattie will be happy to pack a nice lunch for all of us."

The practical side of Catherine emerged. "What are we going to do for sleeping arrangements? There's only one bed there, if that hasn't been done away with."

"Don't you worry about a thing. We can borrow two beds and set them up in the dining room. That space should be empty because you brought the dining room set down here. I'm going up to collect Annie so I can get started making plans."

"Seems to me you've already been making plans."

"Catherine, you know as well as I that we must take the opportunity when it presents itself."

Catherine smiled and shook her head. "Go up and collect Annie while I decide how I got talked into this."

Carolyn was almost out the kitchen door. "You won't be sorry," she called back.

Catherine wasn't so sure.

Chapter 4

The four days before their departure was a whirlwind of preparations. Mattie agreed to take care of the place until Catherine returned.

Catherine was pinning on her hat when Mattie appeared in the foyer. "I done packed this picnic basket full for you ladies and the little ones."

"Thank you. I wish I could tell you when to expect me back, but I'm not sure myself. I hate to not be here when a letter from Patrick arrives. I've written the address of where I will be on this stamped envelope. I would like to have you put his letter inside this envelope and send it to me in the mail. I'll leave it right here on this side table."

"Yessum, jus' as soon as it comes." She cocked her head to one side. "Miz' Catherine. Are you feelin' all right? I been worried 'cause you done looked a bit peaked as of late."

Catherine picked up her gloves and pocketbook before she took the basket Mattie offered. "Now, don't you worry about me. My tummy has been a little upset. This will be my first trip back to Berryville in almost two years."

"May be what you needs with Mistah' Patrick gone."

Leaving the porch, Catherine turned and waved before she started down the brick walk. With a wistful sigh, she passed her closed hat shop that sat thirty yards in front and to the side of the main house.

That small hat shop held the Burke family until Patrick's father had an imposing, more socially acceptable, house built on K Street in Washington. The stone house was deeded to Patrick and held sentimental value. Rather than tear it down, he had the larger brick house built behind it.

After they were married, Patrick offered the quaint house to Catherine for a hat shop. It was ideal. Many hours were spent in the shop while Patrick resumed medical studies. She hadn't wanted to close it, but with the war and Patrick leaving, and her not feeling well, it seemed the practical path to take.

The crisp morning air was refreshing. Catherine took some deep breaths before setting off on her two block walk to the trolley stop. A taxi would have been preferable. She was watching her pennies just in case this war went on longer than the country hoped.

In the heart of D.C., Carolyn and Annie joined her on the trolley that was headed for Alexandria.

"I don't think I slept two hours during the night I was so excited about this trip," Carolyn said as she settled herself next to Catherine with Annie sandwiched between them. "Are you all right? You look a little green around the gills."

"My stomach is not as settled as I'd like. I brought some mints. Poor Mattie held a doleful look when I left. I tried to assure her that I was fine."

"Let me hold the food basket," Carolyn offered. "There's bound to be a smell wafting up and that wouldn't help your queasiness."

Catherine gladly handed it over for Carolyn to carry.

When they reached the Alexandria station, Catherine hurried off the trolley car and headed to the women's private area. Once inside, she locked the door and went through a session of relieving her stomach and ending up with dry heaves. When that finished, she washed her face with cold water and felt well enough to meet up with Carolyn, who was waiting on the train platform.

Annie was being entertained watching men piling baggage on a dolly. The iron wheels made a grinding sound on the wooden platform as they rolled along with the heavy load.

"The porter handled our bags for us. I gave him a couple of dimes. Do you feel better?" Carolyn asked.

"Much. Mornings are worse with the stomach upheaval. Once I've thrown up, all settles down and I'm back to normal. Where's Elizabeth? The train is supposed to leave in fifteen minutes."

"She'll be here. She said she was stunned when you told her the reason you were going to see the doctor. Now, she's concerned also."

"That wasn't my intention."

Carolyn looked around at the crowded platform and into the surrounding parking lot filled with carriages, wagons and automobiles, some with tops and some without. "Isn't that her father's Tin Lizzy pulling up?"

Catherine looked in the direction Carolyn pointed. "It could be. They all look alike to me."

"Here, you watch Annie and the picnic basket. I'll help Elizabeth with Matthew and her cases."

"Cases?" asked Catherine.

"I know she'll have more than one. Elizabeth likes to be prepared."

"Over prepared," muttered Catherine as she watched Carolyn hurry toward a black Model T Ford.

Elizabeth's father took two more small satchels out of the back seat of the car. He handed them to Carolyn, patted Matthew on the top of his capped head, waved to the women, and climbed back into the front seat.

Carolyn took the heavier suitcase from Elizabeth and handed her one of the smaller satchels. Elizabeth took Matthew's hand and they came to where Catherine and Annie waited.

"You look fetching, Elizabeth. Is that a new wrap?" asked Catherine.

"Yes, it is. I want Matthew and I to look our best when we go to see Andrew's parents. They're probably still trying to absorb the fact that Andrew married me. I'm sure they hoped for a pristine wife for him. And, there's his peevish sister, Ruth. I doubt if she's changed. She'll scrutinize every stitch I have on."

"I doubt if much has changed since we were in Berryville last," remarked Catherine. "Don't put yourself down, Elizabeth. I'm glad you're with us."

Carolyn stood up after retying Annie's velvet bonnet. "Admit it, Catherine. Wasn't this a good idea of mine?"

"The proof is in the pudding. We haven't even left Alexandria."

The conductor called, "All aboard for Fairfax, Leesburg, points west and all little burgs in between."

"A man with a sense of humor," acknowledged Catherine. She looked around at the others, who had gathered the two little ones in their arms. She wondered what this endeavor held in store for her.

**

After an uneventful but tiring ride, the train pulled into the Bluemont station where the three women entered the small, red-roofed depot. An old, pot-bellied stove kept a corner of the room warm. Inns in the village were quiet, a contrast to the seasonal summer vacationers who opted for the cooler temperatures in the mountains rather than the oppressive humid days in Washington.

There were few passengers to take the long car down off the mountain to Berryville, ten miles away. That was good news to the three women because the children were getting restless and cranky after the long train ride. It was close to three o'clock in the afternoon, still enough light to get

31

settled into the apartment over the hat shop before dusk set in.

"Is Mr. Marks still driving the big car?" Catherine asked the short, burly station master. The man had been eyeing them ever since they stepped off the train.

"Ain't you the lady who used to live in Berryville?"

"Yes, I'm Catherine Burke." Because Elizabeth had taken the train to Washington many times within the past year, Catherine nodded in Elizabeth's direction. "You probably also remember Mrs. Caldwell."

"Ain't likely to fergit' a pretty face." He turned his attention to Elizabeth. "Heard you and Captain Caldwell got married a few months ago. That yer' son?" He cocked an inquisitive eyebrow.

Matthew was busy trying to pull a log out of the wood box.

The man was entirely too nosey, which annoyed Elizabeth. "It's Major Caldwell. And yes, that," pointing to Matthew, "is the major's and my son!" She rose from her seat. "Catherine, I'm going to take Matthew outside so he can run and stretch his legs."

Carolyn was off her chair with haste. "I'll come with you. Let me button up Annie's coat. It will do the children good to get some fresh air before we take the ride into town."

They left Catherine with the station master.

"Spunky little thing, ain't she?"

The man was irritating. "I don't believe you told me if Mr. Marks is still driving the long car into Berryville."

"They gave up the twelve-passenger car. Not makin' money. But he's got another that'll fit ya' all in."

He glanced up at the clock on the wall. "Should be here in another fifteen minutes or so. Never know with Herbert."

How reassuring, thought Catherine. The room was getting warm and she was beginning to feel uncomfortable. Pulling a mint from her pocket, she popped it into her mouth hoping to stave off the unrest that was forming in the pit of her stomach.

Carolyn opened the door and poked her head in. "Mr. Marks is driving up the road now." She took a second look at Catherine. "Are you feeling all right?"

"I'll be fine once we're on our way."

"Let me carry your things. Elizabeth is watching the children. I'll feel better once you see Dr. Hawthorne."

As will I, Catherine voiced to herself.

**

By the time they arrived in Berryville, Annie and Matthew were at the whiney stage, the mothers were at the frustration stage, and Catherine wasn't feeling well. They allowed Mr. Marks to carry the luggage up to the apartment, which he gladly did for a healthy tip.

It took so much time to get everyone up the short set of steps and off the stoop that the women were sure the whole town knew they were back. And, if not then, it wouldn't be but a short time for Herbert Marks to get the word out. Of course, they most likely hadn't escaped the scrutiny of Lavinia Talley, the editor's wife who lived catty-corner from the hat shop. She was known to be the gossip-peddler. Any happening in a small town is big news.

They gathered in the foyer before mounting the wide staircase that led up to the apartment.

"Catherine, you are to go into bed and lie down," Carolyn ordered. "Elizabeth and I will take the children over to the general store for supplies. Is there anything special you need?"

"I am exhausted, Carolyn. Get something for dinner and breakfast and we'll make a list tomorrow."

She willingly went in to lie on the bed even though the whole place needed a good airing.

Carolyn looked in the bedroom doorway before she left to be sure Catherine was resting. "This musty smell isn't going to make you throw up is it? I'll open a window when I get back."

Catherine waved a weary hand to signal she could tolerate the stale odor.

Once the din of them getting ready to go, the clomping down the wooden stairs stopped, and the front door closed, Catherine breathed a sigh of relief. Her stomach had calmed down. She settled into the stillness of the room. The noisy group would be gone for at least half an hour and she would luxuriate in the peace and quiet. Edginess was so unlike her, but that's how she felt and there didn't seem to be anything she could do about it.

An hour later, she was awakened on their return by the commotion in the downstairs foyer. She arose from the bed, smoothed her dress and reset the clip in her honey-colored hair.

Elizabeth rapped on the door before she opened it. "Are you feeling better, Catherine?"

"Yes, I had a good nap."

"I hope the children aren't upsetting you. They'll settle down once they're fed and bathed. Carolyn is fixing their dinner now. We'll get them taken care of and then the three of us can have some peaceful moments."

"What are we going to do about sleeping arrangements?"

"Carolyn has it all figured out for tonight. She will sleep with you. I'll sleep on the chintz sofa, and we'll make pallets for the children on the floor in the living room where I'll be. They'll be nice and warm near the fireplace."

Catherine smiled. "Carolyn said I wasn't to worry about a thing."

In the low-ceilinged kitchen, they found Carolyn busy around the stove in a bib apron. The two little ones were stuffing their mouths with mashed potatoes.

"I fried up some bacon for them and they can have some applesauce once they're through playing with their potatoes."

"It's a good thing we're giving them a bath because they're a mess. You should have kept an eye on them," admonished Elizabeth.

"It all washes off," came Carolyn's reply. "It will help to get some of the ginger out of them. They'll fall into a deep sleep when we put them down."

"I suppose you're right. I just hate all that icky stuff."

Carolyn turned the meat in the frying pan and shook her head. "You could never be a nurse. You can wash off the plates and utensils for our dinner. I've got pork chops and potatoes and we can open a can of corn."

"I'll take care of the dishes," offered Catherine. "The nap did me a lot of good."

"I'm glad." Elizabeth sent a genuine smile Catherine's way. "I'll set out the children's nightclothes. Carolyn, when you're ready, I'll need your help to lift the ham boiler off the stove and pour the hot water into the tub."

Catherine was quick to offer, "I can help you with that."

Carolyn did an abrupt about-face from the stove and shook a spoon in Catherine's direction. "What are you thinking of? You are not to do any heavy lifting or heavy work until you see Dr. Hawthorne!"

Catherine sent a disgruntled look but acquiesced. "All right. I'll settle for the dishes."

Chapter 5

This was the morning Catherine was going to see the doctor. Her nerves felt like pins and needles.

She could hear the children's clamor emanating from the kitchen and the muffled voices of Carolyn and Elizabeth preparing for the day.

Catherine rose and dressed as simply as she could in a cotton dress. She was sitting on the edge of the bed when Carolyn knocked on the door.

"Come in." She looked up and smiled at her friend. "I was just sitting here thinking about Patrick. Maybe I should have told him. Then, I thought, maybe it is good I didn't because, if I lose this baby, he doesn't have to worry about me."

Carolyn came to sit beside her. "Catherine, let's wait and see what Dr. Hawthorne has to say. Do you think you can down some tea and toast?"

"Right now my stomach feels pretty good."

Carolyn offered her friend a hand up. "Then let's go face the music of the two little ones in the kitchen. Elizabeth is going to turn the dining room into a playroom for them so they don't have free rein of the place."

"A splendid idea."

**

The Hawthorne House looked the same. It was still the massive red brick building with five

37

chimneys jutting out of the roof. Catherine and Carolyn walked up the three steps from the main street and entered the double doors that led to a wide, wooden, tier of stairs leading to the first floor of the building. The doctor's waiting room was to the right. His office and examining rooms to the left. When they entered the reception room, every footfall left a clunking sound on the wood floor that echoed through the cavernous room.

Carolyn had lived and worked here as a nurse so she knew every nook and cranny. The role of visitor made her feel like a stranger.

She and Catherine walked to the unfamiliar receptionist.

"Yes?" The woman looked to be in her forties. She was average height and size with black hair and an air of authority.

"Good morning. We would like to see Dr. Hawthorne," said Catherine.

"Both of you?" The woman raised an eyebrow.

Carolyn butted in before Catherine could respond, "It's a social call."

"Dr. Hawthorne is very busy. He doesn't have time for social calls in the morning."

Carolyn took an instant dislike to the receptionist. "As we are the only ones in the waiting room, I'm sure he can spare ten minutes."

The woman gave a heavy sigh before she pushed her chair back and stood behind the desk. "Your names, please."

"Mrs. Catherine Burke and Mrs. Carolyn Thomas."

The woman huffed to the door. "I shall give him the message."

She returned shortly with the physician at her heels.

"Young ladies, what a pleasure to see you both! Come into my office."

Once inside, Carolyn said, "Dr. Hawthorne, we don't want to keep you from your work. I talked Catherine into coming to see you and neither of us want the word to get out."

"I guessed this was more than a social call. Have a seat and tell me what's troubling you young ladies. What is the problem?"

"The problem is me. I feel jumpy as a cat," spoke Catherine. "I believe I am going to have a baby and I'm not sure all is well."

It was time for Carolyn to step aside. "If you two don't mind, I'll stay in the waiting room."

"I have a better idea," the doctor suggested, "Mrs. Hawthorne is upstairs, Carolyn. Why don't you go up and visit with her. She'll want to hear all about your little one and what has been going on in your life."

"That would be grand. Catherine come up and get me if I'm not down here when you're through." She was out the door and on her way to see Grace Hawthorne.

Catherine settled into a straight chair as the physician took a seat at the desk. She explained not only her physical complaints, but also the fact that

Patrick had gone to Europe and she had not told him she suspected a baby was on the way.

He listened patiently. "Once I've performed the examination, then we'll know for sure."

When he was through, he made notes.

Catherine returned to the chair she'd vacated and sat as still as a mouse.

"I'm keeping this information separate from your chart, as you prefer. If it stays with me, then the word will not get out."

He stopped, as if in thought, before he continued, "I will document the reason for your visit as female problems to satisfy the secretary's need for an explanation for the records."

"Thank you."

They sat facing each other. Catherine perched on the edge of her chair. He leaned forward taking her into his confidence. "You are definitely with child. The morning sickness is normal and so is the edginess. These usually subside after the third or fourth month. The spotting, on the other hand, is not a normal course, although there are cases where this clears without further problems. But, I have to be honest with you and tell you, in my experience, most of these cases end up in a miscarriage."

Catherine sat back in her chair and buried her face in her hands. He allowed her time to compose herself. With effort, she swallowed the lump that had jumped into her throat. Her voice was close to a whisper. "It is what I suspected and didn't want to hear."

"Sometimes the egg just doesn't settle properly. I look at miscarriages as the body's way of getting rid of what is not perfect."

"But, I am twenty-six and my heart cries for a child."

He placed a sympathetic hand on her shoulder. "I understand. Let's look at the bright side, which is that you are still young. If this doesn't work out, there will be other chances. As of yet this baby is still stable. I have seen many women who have miscarried go on to produce healthy offspring." He gave a wry smile. "Sometimes more than they hoped for."

"I'm afraid Patrick won't return from that awful war," she blurted out and tears burst forth.

He sat back in his chair. "And, now we come to the crux of the situation. What makes you think he will not return? Medical people are kept out of the fray because neither side wants to lose them. Doctors are there to save lives."

She sniffed and dabbed the tears away. "I just haven't been able to put the worry out of my mind. See how I'm acting? This is not like me at all."

"No it isn't. You were always the practical one. When a woman is carrying a baby, her emotions sometimes surprise herself."

A wan smile appeared on Catherine's pleasant face. "What you are telling me is that I must wait and see and be prepared for what may happen."

"I can't give you better advice. I have no medicine that will help. Go about your usual tasks except for heavy lifting. How long will you be in town?"

"I'm not sure. At least a week and maybe two."

"While you're here, if you experience any cramping, I want to see you. When you go back to Washington, I'll send my information with you for your doctor."

"I haven't a physician there."

"Then you need to line one up as quickly as possible when you return."

"Of course. Thank you, Dr. Hawthorne. I'll tell Carolyn and Elizabeth what we've discussed."

"Mrs. Caldwell is here, also?"

"Yes, we're staying in my old apartment."

He laughed. "That should keep Mrs. Talley busy." He rose from his chair. "It's nice to have you back in town. Perhaps you three girls can have lunch with Mrs. Hawthorne at the Battletown Inn. Grace would appreciate it."

She rose from the chair and patted her face to erase signs of tears. "How can I arrange to pay you without the secretary involved?"

"This visit was a social call, remember? There is no fee."

Catherine took his hand in hers. "I shall agree to this one time. And, thank you again. I feel somewhat relieved. Now, I'd better hurry upstairs and rescue your wife. Carolyn can sometimes get carried away if she gets on the topic of the Suffragette Movement."

"I admire her energy and zeal," he responded. "Please tell her that I miss having her as my right hand nurse."

"I will." She left the room in search of Carolyn.

**

In the apartment, Elizabeth was boiling diapers in the ham boiler. She ran to the top of the stairs when she heard them come in the front door. "I'm glad to see you back," she called over the stair railing. "You were gone longer than I expected."

They came up the stairs.

"We visited with Mrs. Hawthorne and ran into Irene Butler opening her dress shop."

"Wait until I tell you about the morning I've had!"

"Let's have some tea. The kitchen is warm and cozy," said Carolyn. "The damp air outside sent a chill to the bone. Where are the children?"

"Playing in that area I fixed up. It works well."

All three took a seat at the table, where Elizabeth placed a bowl of vegetable soup and a cup of hot tea before them.

"Tell us about your morning," encouraged Catherine.

"Not until you tell me about what Dr. Hawthorne had to say. It has been on my mind ever since you left."

Catherine gave her the same information she had shared with Carolyn.

Elizabeth was remorseful. "So there is nothing we can do?"

"Pray a lot." Catherine tried to be upbeat. "You know that I am a firm believer in Providence."

"Keep that thought in mind," advised Carolyn. "By the way, Elizabeth, sour little Irene Butler wanted you to know that she has not forgiven you for closing the hat shop. She has had to employ Mary Lee for weddings."

"That sounds like Irene. She should be happy because Mary Lee was the creative one."

"Mary Lee doesn't like to come into town so Irene has had to travel out to the Mitchell estate."

Elizabeth laughed. "Hooray for Mary Lee."

Catherine took a spoonful of soup. "So, tell us about your morning."

Elizabeth sat her teacup back on its saucer. "I just got the children cordoned off in the dining room when that handle in the door clanged. I went down to answer it. Surprise, surprise, there was Lavinia Talley, as round and plump as ever, grinning from ear to ear."

"'Mrs. Talley, how nice to see you,' said I, while gritting my teeth.

"I heard you girls were in town and I wanted to come and say hello."

"I would invite you in but Carolyn and Catherine aren't here."

"They aren't? You just got in last evening."

Elizabeth paused in telling her story. "The woman never realizes she gives herself away. Anyway, I told her that you had both gone up to visit the Hawthornes."

"I'll bet that piqued her interest. I can see one questioning eyebrow raised over those beady eyes right now." Carolyn was not one to mince words.

Elizabeth continued, "Mrs. Talley thought it was too early in the day to go calling, especially when the doctor has office hours. I told her we expected to be here only for the week and you wanted to see Mrs. Hawthorne."

"Thinking on your feet," Catherine said with approval.

"Then I heard the children putting up a fuss. I told her I was sorry but I had to go up and check on the little ones. She actually stuck her foot in the door. 'I understand you and Major Caldwell have a son, and only after five months of marriage.' I could have slapped her."

Carolyn dropped her spoon. "She actually said that?"

"You know Mrs. Talley, Carolyn. Tact is not one of her shining virtues. The children really started to howl at that point. I said I would tell you both she stopped by, and I closed the door. She was quick enough to pull her foot away."

"It's a good thing we're only here for a visit," said Catherine. "Thank you for the lunch,

Elizabeth. You two will have to excuse me because I need to go lie down. I'm tired."

"You should be," agreed Carolyn before turning to Elizabeth. "We have to get those diapers hung up and dried out before we run out of clean ones. Did you string the clothesline in the living room?"

"You'll have to help me. I'm not tall enough. I couldn't do it myself without climbing up on a stool."

"Catherine, you go lie down. We'll feed the children some lunch and try to quiet them for a nap. I didn't realize we'd been gone so long this morning."

Catherine headed for the bedroom.

A ruckus erupted from the playroom causing the mothers to rush to their children's aid. Annie was screaming and crying because Matthew was trying his best to pull a stuffed toy away from her.

A harried Elizabeth looked at Carolyn. "You wondered why I was glad to see you get back here?"

Chapter 6

The next day Carolyn was to visit her family. It had been over a year since she had seen them. Her younger brothers were coming into town early and she wanted to be ready. She glanced out the upstairs window that overlooked the main street watching for their wagon.

Elizabeth was folding diapers. "When will you be back?"

"Tomorrow evening. We'll just be gone overnight."

"What will I do if Catherine has problems?"

"Use that pretty head of yours." Then she saw the tense look on Elizabeth's face. "You can go to the hotel and have someone run up to get Doctor Hawthorne if it's necessary."

Elizabeth wasn't so sure. "You're a nurse, you would know what to do."

"What I would do is just what I told you. Now, I've got to hurry. I see the wagon coming around the corner."

Elizabeth pulled back the curtain and peeked out the window. "My goodness, those teenage brothers of yours look full-grown."

When Carolyn got to the street, her brother, Jack, hopped out of the wagon and pulled her into a bear hug.

"Jack, you're crushing me." He let go with a devilish grin on his face. "I think you're a foot taller than when I last saw you. Look at that face full of hair." She fingered his whiskers.

He pointed to his brother who was leaving the wagon seat. "Yeh', me and Harry are tryin' to grow beards. Ma ain't too pleased about 'em."

"They'll be warm for winter," Carolyn acknowledged.

Harry was less boisterous than Jack. He walked up and hugged Carolyn before he hunched down to see Ann Catherine, who was hiding behind her mother's skirt. "This must be your little girl."

Carolyn had almost forgotten her child. She took her in her arms. "Annie, these are your uncles."

The child looked uncertain. Harry gave her a gentle touch on the cheek with one rough finger.

"Jack, you get 'em in the wagon and turn it around while I pick up a couple of things Ma wants at the store."

"C'mon, Carolyn. Climb up and I'll lift Annie," Jack ordered.

"Be careful with her. She isn't used to being manhandled."

"You mean that big army daddy of hers don't toss her around?"

Carolyn climbed up into the wagon seat. "Her big army daddy is gentle and he's been gone for over three weeks."

"Harry and me thought about signin' up, but Pa wouldn't hear of it. Said we were needed 'round the farm. Here she is." He laughed as he made the pretense of throwing Annie up for Carolyn to catch.

"You may have grown a foot taller and old enough to sprout a beard, but you still act like a kid. You'd better get this wagon turned around before Harry comes." She cuddled her child close. "What a big girl you are. You didn't even cry. Just wait until my sisters see you, they'll spoil you to death." Carolyn kissed her soft cheek. Annie buried herself against her mother's chest.

Elizabeth watched from the apartment window wondering what it was like to have brothers and sisters. She looked over at Matthew playing with some wooden blocks. Would he grow up an only child? How sad for him, she thought.

Catherine came out with her blue chenille housecoat wrapped around her. "Has Carolyn gone?"

"They're pulling out now. Come to the window and we'll wave."

Catherine looked out as Carolyn looked up at the window. She must have seen them looking down because she gave a big wave of her hand.

"How do you feel, Catherine?"

"Quite good this morning. I slept well and my stomach is not in an upheaval."

"That's good to hear. Can I fix you some poached eggs and toast?"

"I'll try the toast. I can do it myself. You stay and play with Matthew."

"He's happy throwing the blocks around. I can use a cup of tea."

"Good. Come and keep me company."

They sat at the table eating toast and drinking tea.

"When do you think we should visit Mary Lee?" Elizabeth asked.

"I was thinking we could go out today while Carolyn is gone. You will want to see Andrew's family one day, and Carolyn wants to go with you. If we're only staying the week, it doesn't give much time."

"What if something happens on the way going or coming back? Matthew will be with us and I'll have two to worry about."

Catherine relaxed in her chair. "I'm not concerned, Elizabeth. Dr. Hawthorne said to go about my normal business. You've hit enough bumps in the road to know they smooth out."

"This is supposed to be a rejuvenating trip. So far, I haven't been brimming with enthusiasm."

Catherine smiled. "Too much of Lavinia Talley. It was good to talk with Doctor Hawthorne, yesterday. At least I know what to expect. Once you get your visit with Andrew's family over with, you'll feel better, too."

"I hope you're right about that." She sat her teacup down. "Let's go see Mary Lee. She brightens everyone's day."

**

Mary Lee Graves, now married and living on the Mitchell estate, was shooing a calico cat out her cottage door when the buggy Elizabeth was driving came up the dirt lane. She squinted in the late October sun. Must be someone going to the big house, she thought. She turned to go back inside when she heard, "Mary Lee!"

The buggy came closer. As soon as she saw it was Elizabeth and Catherine waving their arms, she ran to meet them.

"Oh, my goodness! Never did I 'spect to see you!" She wiped a happy tear from her blue eyes with the back of her hand and brushed back strands of red hair from her freckled cheek. "Miz' Elizabeth, drive that buggy right around the side of the house an' we can tie the horse to the post." She ran ahead of the horse and guided the buggy into place.

Elizabeth threw the reins to Mary Lee, who fastened them to a large T-shaped hitching post.

Elizabeth jumped to the ground and hugged Mary Lee with all her might.

"Elizabeth, I'll hand Matthew down to you," called Catherine.

"No, Catherine. He can climb down by himself. I'll be here to make sure he doesn't fall."

Mary Lee watched. "Miz' Elizabeth, I ain't never seen your little one, but it ain't hard to tell that he belongs to you."

The proud mother removed Matthew's hat and playfully tousled his blonde hair. "That's exactly what I thought when I first saw him in the orphanage. He's got my coloring…"

51

"But not your size," added Catherine, who had stepped off the buggy and came to join them. She gave Mary Lee a warm hug. "From the glow in your cheeks, I'd say that married life agrees with you."

"Yes, ma'am, 'deed it does. C'mon in. Don't fall over the bushel of apples Robert brought in before he left. They're in the middle of the kitchen floor."

"Robert isn't here?" asked Elizabeth. "I hoped I would see him. And, Catherine wanted to meet him."

"He had to go with Mr. Mitchell to pick out some livestock. He likes the way Robert can spot good cattle and horses. Besides, I've told him so much about the times I worked fer you, Miz' Catherine, in the hat shop, y'know, before you sold it to Miz' Elizabeth, Robert prob'ly thinks he knows you."

Mary Lee held the door open for them to go into the cottage. Catherine had to duck as she entered.

The limestone cottage was like one huge room with a bedroom attached. The kitchen area was separated by a thick wooden beam in the low ceiling. There was a fire going in the fireplace making the interior comfortable.

"You've put up curtains," observed Elizabeth.

"I couldn't stand them bare windows. Robert said he didn't care as long as I didn't put anythin' frilly up."

"Where did you get the material?" asked Catherine.

"They were feed sacks I found in the stables. They wuz' goin' to throw 'em away. Can you imagine that? Anyway, I bleached 'em out. Then Irene Butler gave me that orangey colored braid and that dressed 'em up."

"Irene gave you that trim?" asked Catherine. "She must be mellowing as she ages."

"I helped her with some weddin' hats. I don't think she liked that orange color anyway. I wuz' right pleased to get it 'cause it matches the color in that ugly plaid chair Robert loves."

"It brightens up the place," complimented Elizabeth.

Matthew had crawled up into a rocking chair by the fireplace, rocking back and forth, and fighting to keep his eyes open.

Catherine had been eyeing Matthew while Elizabeth examined the curtains. "Elizabeth, I think your son is going to drop off to sleep."

Elizabeth turned from inspecting Mary Lee's handiwork. She looked over at Matthew. "It's his usual naptime. If you don't mind, Mary Lee, I'll leave him there while you tell us what's been going on around here."

"He's fine. Let's us have some lunch. I baked bread yesterday an' I got roast beef we can slice fer sandwiches. The kettle's already hot fer tea." Mary Lee pushed the bushel of apples out of the way.

"Why don't we peel some of those apples while you fix the sandwiches?" Catherine offered.

"We didn't plan on you having to feed us lunch." She looked at Elizabeth. "I guess we didn't plan on anything."

Elizabeth smiled. "If we didn't get out here today, we might not have been able to see you while we were here."

"I'm right happy you came. I would have felt bad if I heard you came and didn't come to see me." Mary Lee sat two big bowls and two paring knives on the table. "I 'spose I shouldn't let you do this, but I ain't fond of peelin' a whole bushel by myself. I told Robert I wuz' gonna' put up some applesauce an' here he comes with that load."

"He thought he was being helpful," surmised Catherine.

Mary Lee brightened. "I know he did. He's awful good t'me, so I gave him a big kiss and thanked him."

Elizabeth and Catherine rolled up their long sleeves and began peeling the apples, while Mary Lee busied herself getting lunch for the three of them.

"How's Miz' Carolyn?" she asked.

"She came with us and is visiting her family."

"I bet her little girl is growin'."

"That she is," answered Elizabeth. "Carolyn is the one who thought we should come back to Berryville for a visit. We saw our husbands off to the war in Europe."

Mary Lee froze. She turned from cutting the bread. "All three of 'em?"

"Andrew and Asa had to go because the army ordered them to."

"What about yer husband, Mister Patrick? I thought he was goin' to start doctorin'."

Catherine sighed, set down the knife and looked at Mary Lee. "So did I. He feels he will gain much experience to help him when he comes back and starts practicing in our country."

"How do you feel about it Miz' Catherine?"

"I wasn't pleased, but I believe I have learned to accept the fact that he's gone."

"And, he will be comin' back," said Mary Lee with finality.

"He will be coming back," agreed Catherine with renewed spirit.

Mary Lee turned her attention back to making sandwiches and Catherine picked up an apple.

Elizabeth was chopping one into the bowl. "Mary Lee, do you remember when we came here with Robert the first time?"

"Do I! You met Major Caldwell that day. We had that picnic up under the oak tree and you didn't even invite him to join us."

"He was rather bold to just come and introduce himself to me while I was waiting for you and Robert."

"Must have seen something he liked," teased Catherine.

"Miz" Elizabeth said there was no way she was gettin' sweet on a man agin'. Look what

55

happened. She ended up marryin' him." They all laughed. "You been out to see the Caldwells?"

She brought a plate of sandwiches to the table while Elizabeth and Catherine set aside their knives and bowls of peeled apples.

"I'm dreading it, but I know I have to go. I'm hoping Carolyn will come with me. She nursed Mrs. Caldwell back to health, so I'm sure they will be glad to see her."

"They will be glad to see you also, Elizabeth," said Catherine.

Mary Lee poured tea into mugs before taking a seat at the table. "I'll say thanks," she said and they joined hands. "Thank you, Lord, for these friends and this food we are about to eat. Please keep the ladies' men safe over there in Europe. Amen."

Catherine and Elizabeth looked at each other under raised eyelids. "Amen," they said.

"Mary Lee, do you like living on the farm?" asked Catherine.

"Oh, I do. It's so big that I can walk all over the place and never leave home. I don't have to worry about havin' food or a warm house. "

Elizabeth was about to take a bite of her roast beef sandwich. "Don't you miss working in the hat shop and living in town? I think I would be lonely living out here. I'm happy to be back in the city."

"You were born and raised in the city," said Catherine. "I'm sure that makes a difference."

"What about you, Miz' Catherine? You live in the city and you wuz' raised in Berryville."

Catherine gave a weak smile. "I made the decision to live where my husband lives, so I have to be satisfied with that. Do I get homesick? Many times." She absently stirred her spoon in the tea.

"What about yer' hat shop in Georgetown?"

"I closed it down. I intend to reopen once the war is over."

Mary Lee's sweet round face took on a concerned look. "I'm sorry 'bout your men bein' gone. I hope Robert don't have to go."

Catherine patted her hand. "I think Robert is safe. We need people on the farms to keep food on the table."

Mary Lee pushed her chair back and stood up. "I don't want to hear no more of this troublin' talk. I made some apple grunt. Once we finish that I'm goin' to show you a quilt I'm makin' fer Christmas. It's a surprise fer Robert."

Elizabeth was leery. "Do you think Robert will appreciate a quilt?"

"He will this one. It looks like geese flyin'."

Catherine and Elizabeth laughed aloud.

Matthew awoke with a start and let out a cry. Elizabeth hurried in to comfort him and brought him to the table.

"Miz' Elizabeth, do you think Matthew could eat some of this apple dessert?"

"He'll love it. I'll feed him from my plate."

"How 'bout a cup of milk fer him, too?"

"That is perfect. We'll be all set for our trip back to town."

After they finished eating, Mary Lee brought out the quilt she had started. "I found an ol' quilt rack up in the barn that had a piece missin', but Sam, he's a hired man over at the farm, he's real good with wood, and he fixed it up fer' me."

"Isn't Robert going to see you working on it?" asked Catherine.

"I'm goin' to set the rack up in that shed out back. Robert don't never go in there. I figure I can have it done before Christmas."

"Where did you get this material?" asked Elizabeth, fingering the quilt.

"Miz' Butler. 'Course ya' know, she was in a bind to get them weddin' hats done right."

"I'd say you made a good bargain," said Elizabeth. "Must have been for an influential family."

"Fact is, it was some niece of some big name in the county. She came all the way from New York City to be married here in Clarke County."

"I can't imagine why," came Elizabeth's reply.

Catherine chuckled. "We all have our idiosyncrasies."

Mary Lee folded up the small piece of quilt and shook her head. "You and Miz' Elizabeth like usin' them big words."

"We like to keep in practice," quipped Catherine. It was good to feel lighthearted.

"Guess who came to see what was going on after we came to town?" asked Elizabeth.

Mary Lee shoved the box back under the bed with her foot. "I don't need to guess. It was most likely that ol' Miz' Talley."

"Catherine and Carolyn had gone to visit the Hawthornes. I stayed to watch Annie and Matthew. Lavinia came by and started cranking that noisy handle in the door. I tried to be nice at first, but I could hear the children fussing upstairs, and I needed to see what they were up to. I almost slammed her foot in the door."

Mary Lee laughed. "She's got to stick her nose everywhere it don't belong. I don't miss that part of livin' in town."

"We had better be on our way, Elizabeth, before the evening sets in. Mr. Hardesty will be looking for us to return the buggy to the livery stable."

"Let me pack up some oatmeal cookies," offered Mary Lee. "Your young one might get hungry before you get back to town. I'm sendin' some popcorn ears, too."

Elizabeth unhitched the horse and drove the buggy around to the front of the cottage. She helped Matthew climb up onto the seat while Catherine said goodbye to Mary Lee.

Then it was Elizabeth's turn to give her friend a parting hug before she climbed up beside

Matthew and Catherine. "Mary Lee, I am pleased to see you well and happy."

"It was so good to visit with you and Miz' Catherine. Maybe you'll come agin'."

"We will if we get back this way."

Elizabeth flicked the reins and the horse started off down the lane. They waved at Mary Lee as they rode away.

When they turned onto the main road, Elizabeth looked over at Catherine. "You didn't even tell Mary Lee you are expecting a baby."

"No, Elizabeth. I didn't see the need until I know all is well."

"I think it will be. You seem so much improved since we left Washington."

"It could be I am more at ease knowing Dr. Hawthorne is close at hand," replied Catherine.

Chapter 7

Carolyn was her usual energetic self when she and Annie returned from spending time with her family. Her mother sent a small, white, iron bed for the children that her brothers hauled back in the wagon. Before they left, they set it up in the dining room.

The three women were sitting at the small table in the kitchen in the evening. The children were asleep.

"I'm sorry you'll still have to sleep on the couch, Elizabeth, but I was happy to get the bed for the little ones. I wish we could have stayed a couple more days, but Annie was overwhelmed with all the attention and hub-bub. My house is never quiet. Even at night there's someone snoring. My mother sent a box of jam, pickles, bacon, ham and eggs."

"Good," said a pleased Catherine. "Add the cookies and popcorn Mary Lee gave us and we'll save money."

"Renting that horse and buggy from the livery stable was expensive," chimed in Elizabeth.

"I'll bet it was more comfortable than jostling around in that farm wagon. My bones still hurt. When we go to Red Gate Farm, you should ask the Caldwells to send a car."

Elizabeth had moved to the stove where she was starting to brew tea. She turned. "For heaven's sake, Carolyn, I couldn't do that."

"Why not?"

Catherine was quick to answer. "It would be an imposition."

"I don't see why. When I took care of Andrew's mother, Mr. Caldwell told me if I ever needed anything to let him know," came Carolyn's reply.

"Then you call him," said Elizabeth.

"I'm not sure they have a telephone."

"So, how did you expect me to contact them?" asked a perturbed Elizabeth.

Carolyn rolled the thought around in her mind for a few seconds. "We can send a boy from the hotel."

"You can send a boy from the hotel," retorted Elizabeth.

Catherine pushed her chair from the table. "You can both send a boy from the hotel. I'm going to bed."

They looked at her. "Are you feeling all right?" asked Carolyn.

"I'm just tired," she answered.

But Catherine wasn't feeling all right. Her back ached and there was a pressure feeling she had never experienced before. She went into the bathroom to brush her teeth and wash up. It was then she felt something warm and sticky oozing from her body.

She checked and almost fainted at the sight of bright red blood in her underwear. "Carolyn!" she shouted and stood stock still.

Carolyn came on the run. She saw the stricken look on Catherine's face. There were bright red spots on the floor. "Elizabeth, we need Dr. Hawthorne," she called.

Elizabeth ran to the bathroom. She took one look, exclaimed, "Oh, no!" and headed for the stairs, donning her coat in the process, before dashing out the door.

Carolyn yanked some diapers off the line in the living room and folded them into a thick padding while guiding Catherine to the bed. "I'm going to fold this padding under you to protect the bed. You lie still until the doctor gets here."

Catherine was shaking. "I'm not going to cry," she said. "I don't know what's happening, but I am not going to cry."

Carolyn knew what was happening. She had witnessed it before. Catherine was in danger of losing her baby and a lot of blood in the process. She assumed her nurse's stoic and calming countenance. "We have to wait to see what the doctor has to say."

Although, in her heart, she was sure he would not be able to change the course of this awful situation.

She laid another blanket over Catherine for extra warmth.

Within fifteen minutes, Dr. Hawthorne was at the bedside. He didn't ask any questions.

"Catherine, I'm going to take you to the Hawthorne House. I need to keep an eye on the bleeding. Carolyn, can you come with us?"

"Of course. Elizabeth is here with the children."

After settling Catherine into the back seat of the Model T, just like the taxies in Washington, they started off to go two blocks to the Hawthorne House.

The moon was bright. With a heavy heart, Elizabeth watched from the upstairs window as they motored away. She couldn't stop the tears that rolled down her cheeks as she said a silent prayer. She checked the children, who had slept through the whole ordeal. They were still fast asleep.

The thought of Andrew flashed into her mind. Why hadn't she had any word? It was the beginning of November. They should have heard something by now, but no information had come. Elizabeth dropped onto the chintz sofa and hoped for sleep.

The next morning Carolyn returned to the upstairs apartment around ten o'clock. Elizabeth was cleaning up the breakfast dishes and soaking beans to bake with ham for dinner. When Carolyn walked into the kitchen, Elizabeth gave her a warm hug. "You look exhausted," she said. "How is Catherine?"

"Heartbroken, she lost the baby but the bleeding has stopped. Dr. Hawthorne wants her to stay a couple more days to be sure all is fine."

"Do you know if the baby was a boy or a girl?"

Carolyn recalled the long night. "There was such a mess of blood and tissue, we were unable to know. We baptized all of it and then burned it along with the linens in the incinerator."

Elizabeth was horrified. "Oh my good heavens."

"What else could we do? Catherine was groggy so she wasn't aware of what was going on. Doctor Hawthorne had given her some calming medicine."

Elizabeth heaved a heavy sigh. "Do you think she will recover?"

"Catherine is strong. Given time, she'll be back to the Catherine we know and love."

Elizabeth smiled. "Why don't you go in and rest? It's such a pretty day, I planned to take the children out for a walk."

"They won't be able to walk too far without getting tired and you can't carry them."

"I know that. I thought we could walk down to the train station and watch the train loading. They can rest before we start back. It's not that far."

"A good idea." Carolyn yawned. "I'm drained. I'll take up your offer to get some rest. Maybe tomorrow we should make that trip out to your in-laws at Red Gate Farm."

"I suppose so. I'll write a note and ask a boy from the hotel to deliver it."

"Are you going to ask them to send a car?"

"Carolyn, I am not going to sound like a beggar."

"That wouldn't bother me. Besides they wouldn't want word to get around that their daughter-in-law had to hire a conveyance."

"How would they find out?"

"I'll tell Lavinia to have Jeremy put it in the *Courier*."

"You wouldn't!"

"I'm not up for another bouncing ride."

Elizabeth sent a wry look toward her friend. "You write the note and I'll see it gets to Henry, but I don't approve."

"Swallow some pride, Elizabeth. It will get us to and from Red Gate faster."

"Perhaps. Write the note while I get the children ready."

Elizabeth had no sooner got the children off the stoop and onto the sidewalk when Lavinia Talley came waddling, as fast as possible, across the street.

"Oh, my," she twittered. "Such beautiful children. We heard that Carolyn had a lovely little girl. Doesn't she favor her with those coal black eyes and dark hair? She is just too cute for words."

Annie glanced up at the woman and huddled closer to Elizabeth.

"And, this must be the little boy that you and Major Caldwell adopted. Isn't it interesting how closely he resembles you?" Lavinia's expression was one big question mark.

"They matched us well," responded Elizabeth. The nosey woman was not going to get the truth from her. Although Elizabeth was sure the suspicion of her having a child out of wedlock and Andrew not being the real father made the circles of gossip. The fact that Matthew had spent a year in a Catholic orphanage was still a secret.

Lavina wasn't through. "Whatever happened last night? I saw Dr. Hawthorne's car parked. At first I thought it was a call from the hotel, but then I saw him going into your apartment."

And saw the three of them coming out, thought Elizabeth.

"Catherine took ill. The doctor saw fit to have her at the Hawthorne House for a couple of days."

"Oh, dear. What seems to be the problem?"

"He is just observing. Now, if you will excuse me, the children are getting restless to get on with our walk."

"By all means. I was on my way up the street to see Irene Butler."

Spreading the news?

Annie and Matthew had a great time playing in leaves and watching men load barrels, trunks, and crates into rail cars. There were no passengers on this train. The engineer was waiting in the engine cab when he spied Elizabeth and the children. He winked and blew the whistle. It startled the two little ones who screamed and ran to Elizabeth, almost knocking her over.

She pulled them close. "Was that necessary?" she yelled over the noise on the platform.

He grinned and hollered back, "I can't resist when I see a pretty lady."

She gave an unpleasant look but smiled, inwardly. She wasn't the innocent, perky, seventeen-year-old anymore. She was a wife and mother, but it was rather nice to be noticed.

As she and the children neared the apartment, Elizabeth spied Lloyd Pierce, the affable, tall, lanky postman coming down the street. She waved. He waved back with a letter in his hand.

"Miz' Elizabeth, I heard you wuz' back in town. Heard Miz' Catherine and Miz' Carolyn are here, too."

They met in front of the stoop. "We plan on being here only for the week."

"Miz' Talley says your men have been taken into the war."

"Mrs. Talley is right."

"Then I 'spect Miz' Catherine is goin' to be happy to get this letter. Got her address here and the return address is her place in Georgetown. My calculation is that she had a letter sent on from Mr. Burke."

Elizabeth knew he was right and wanted to snatch it out of his hand. "He's Dr. Burke now."

"How about that. You'll see that it gets to her?"

"Just as soon as I can. How are you and Mrs. Pierce?"

"She wishes you were still sellin' hats and jewelry. Says there ain't nothin' much to look at in the general store."

"There's still the jewelry shop in town."

"I can't afford that stuff. Too rich for my blood."

Elizabeth laughed. "Tell Mrs. Pierce that we all say hello."

She hurried the two children into the foyer and called to Carolyn as they were going up the stairs. "Carolyn, I think there is a letter from Patrick!"

Carolyn was bleary-eyed from waking from sleep. "Patrick? Patrick! Are you sure?"

"I'm quite sure. Remember Catherine saying she had given instructions to Mattie to send letters on if any came?"

"Let me see it," Carolyn said and grabbed the letter out of Elizabeth's hand. She took it to the window and held it up to the light. "Maybe we can see what's inside."

Elizabeth snatched it back. "That's Catherine's letter."

Carolyn looked chagrined. "I wasn't going to open it."

"I can run it up to her at the Hawthorne House. Maybe it will lift her spirits," offered Elizabeth.

"Let me run it up," said Carolyn. "I want to hear what he has to say."

Elizabeth stood her ground. "So do I! Someone has to watch the children. You can stay here."

"Compromise," offered Carolyn. "We can see if the Hawthorne twins are home. They can play with Annie and Matthew while we see Catherine. Mrs. Hawthorne said she wanted to see the children."

Elizabeth shook her head in exasperation. "Carolyn, have you no sense of pride?"

"Not when I need something," she answered. "Let's get these two ready and hurry up to see Catherine."

Chapter 8

The next morning the lithe and graceful doctor's wife, Grace Hawthorne, entered Catherine's room with a breakfast tray. "Catherine, I thought you might be up to some oatmeal, toast and tea."

Catherine was sitting in a chair. She had been awake for two hours. "That's kind of you. I'm not sure about the oatmeal. I will enjoy the toast and tea."

"Are you feeling better?"

"Yes. I cried my eyes out, and when Elizabeth and Carolyn came we all cried together, so I guess the tears are gone."

Grace's smile was sympathetic. "But the sadness remains."

Catherine nodded.

Grace set the tray on a low table by Catherine's chair and poured the tea. "The anger, guilt and disappointment will dissolve as your body returns to its normal self. I do understand how you feel, Catherine, for I experienced the same misfortune with my first. I was sure I would never get over it. One year later I was blessed with the twins."

"Your husband says I have two things going for me; I am young enough, and I am capable of carrying a child."

"Thaddeus is right. You have many years ahead of you. Now, I understand you received a letter from Dr. Burke. Is he settled over there?"

"Not quite. The reason Carolyn and Elizabeth both came with the letter was because they have not heard from their husbands and they hoped Patrick had some information. It was good of you and your children to take care of Annie and Matthew while we visited."

"Such delightful little ones," said Grace. "Robert and Rebecca were happy to keep them busy. Before you girls leave, I will take you to dinner at the Battletown Inn. We can let the twins entertain the children here while we have a wonderful gab session. I miss having you young ladies in town."

Catherine grinned. "You can always have a gab session with Mrs. Talley."

Grace had moved to the door. "Do I detect dry humor from the Catherine I know? Lavinia? Wouldn't that set the town on its ear!" She shook her head. "No, I think not."

As soon as Grace left, Catherine pulled Patrick's letter from her pocket.

October 29, 1917

My dearest Catherine,

Finally, after nine days at sea and trouble finding where I was supposed to be, I have settled in for a time and have a few minutes to write to bring you up to date.

Our crossing was without incident, save two days of choppy weather. My stomach did not fare well with the tossing about. I lost a few pounds. I could use some of Mattie's delectable dinners to gain what I lost, but I am healthy and feeling fit so that is what counts. Food is not plentiful here in England, which is understandable as they have been fighting this war for three years. Much of the food comes from the U.S.

I must tell you about Asa and Andrew. I am sure they have not been in a position to write. They were immediately sent to France when we arrived to help build up headquarters for the 26th "Yankee" Division.

I am told the headquarters will be in Neufchateau, a small village in the northeastern part of France. In fact, by the time you receive this letter, suitable facilities should be in place. The troops have been billeted in barns, lofts and stables until supplies arrived.

This will be a training base under the guidance of the French as the Americans are here only to help. Andrew and Asa were both concerned about the conditions and unpreparedness of our boys.

There will be a field hospital set up, but I am unsure if I will be sent there. Here in England, I am helping to fill in and give the attending physicians some rest. There is no immediate danger here. We are getting the maimed who have been treated in the field hospitals and sent here for either recovery or discharge. It would break your heart to see the

*conditions some of these young men have suffered.
Enough of the war.*

*I cannot put into words how much I miss
you, how much I wish you were with me, and how
many times I have questioned myself for leaving
you.*

*I trust you are in good health and that Mattie
is taking good care of you.*

*Please relay to Carolyn and Elizabeth that
Asa and Andrew send their love; their last words
before we parted.*

*I am on duty in fifteen minutes so I must sign
off.*

I adore you with all my heart.

*Your loving husband,
Patrick*

Catherine carefully folded the letter, dried
the few tears that had fallen on it and put it back
into her pocket, satisfied that Patrick was not in
harm's way. She felt good enough to go back to the
apartment but Dr. Hawthorne said one more day.
And, this was the day Elizabeth and Carolyn were
going to take the trip to Red Gate Farm. Catherine
decided it was just as well she stayed right where
she was. Perhaps Grace Hawthorne would break
the monotony of the day by returning for a game
of checkers.

**

The morning sun was a welcome sight as Carolyn and Elizabeth bundled the children into the yellow Packard touring car Mr. Caldwell had sent. The driver was a small, little man who could pass for a jockey with his cap, knickers and riding jacket. He doffed his cap before opening the back doors for his riders to get settled.

"Mornin' ladies. The name is Stuart. I've put the top up for a warmer ride. The day's got a chill to it."

"It does," agreed Carolyn.

They rode in the back seat with the children on their laps.

The car was familiar to Carolyn as it was the same that had taken her from the nursing school in Winchester to her first position as a nurse at Red Gate Farm. Was it possible her life had changed so much in three years? She had worked for Dr. Hawthorne, married Asa and sat holding her sixteen-month-old daughter.

She smiled as she recalled tall, handsome James Anderson driving her in that fancy car with its black leather seats and yellow spoke wheels. Stuart was a far cry from the dashing James; the man who had stolen a piece of her heart. The remembrance of him gave her a start.

"Are you daydreaming?" asked Elizabeth.

"I was thinking about the time I spent taking care of Andrew's mother."

"Someday you'll have to tell me more about it. I must admit I am apprehensive about this visit. I don't know Andrew's parents well. I've only spent a few hours with them and most of that was at the dinner table. After we married, we brought Matthew out to meet his grandparents. The reception was cool. Mr. Caldwell seemed to be more accepting than Andrew's mother."

"Andrew is his mother's favorite. You probably didn't fit the mold. She's nice enough, but there is always that English screen of propriety; we musn't let the guard down. You should be used to that, Elizabeth. Your mother is much the same."

Elizabeth stood Matthew on the floorboards to smooth out her dress. "Don't remind me of my mother. How much longer do we have to go?"

"We're almost to Millwood so it should be about another half-hour."

Matthew was getting restless. Elizabeth pulled a toy from her pocketbook. It was one of those stringed clowns on a ladder. When Matthew squeezed the ladder, the clown jumped up and, when his hand released, the clown fell down.

Annie sat on her mother's lap clapping and laughing at the comical routine.

"I believe girls are easier than boys," remarked Elizabeth. "If Annie was playing with this toy, Matthew would be grabbing for it."

Once at the farm, Stuart got out of the car to open the large, red, iron gate that stood between two stone pillars. They drove through the opening and waited, once again, while he secured the latch.

Up the oak-lined drive they rode to the front steps of the red brick manor.

Carolyn whispered to Elizabeth, "When James first brought me, we had to use the servant's entrance."

The car stopped. Stuart opened the back door. Elizabeth stepped out with Matthew at her side. As she leaned down to get a tote bag, Matthew escaped her hold and started running down the lawn.

Elizabeth was in pursuit. "Matthew come back. Wait for mommy."

Before she could reach him, he stumbled and fell onto a patch of dirt.

She was miffed and concerned at the same time. She shook him. "Look at you. You've got your good suit dirty."

Matthew started to cry and she pulled him close.

"I'm sorry. When mommy tells you to stop, you must stop."

Carolyn arrived on the scene with Annie in her arms. "Is he all right?"

"Yes, but he got his suit dirty and it won't brush off. What are the Caldwells going to think?"

"Probably that he's a healthy, handsome little guy. Be happy he didn't get hurt when he fell. There are more important things in this world than a smudge of soil on a suit."

"I wanted to make a good impression."

"I'm sure you did, running down the front lawn."

Elizabeth had to smile. "You've made your point." She wiped Matthew's tear-stained face and gave him a hug. "Let's go in and see what else is going to happen."

The wide entrance door was opened by Doris, the rotund, colored maid who took care of the first floor.

"Hello, Doris. Remember me?"

"Oh, Miz' Carolyn. We been waitin' fer you."

Carolyn gave her a hug. "This is Annie."

"Hello, sweet child," said Doris. "She looks like you and Major Thomas both, what with those dark eyes and black hair. Jus' wait 'til Ollie spies her."

"I can hardly wait to see Ollie. Is she still the queen of the kitchen?"

"You know she is orderin' everybody aroun' like she owns it."

Elizabeth had stood back holding Matthew's hand.

Carolyn stepped aside. "Elizabeth, I'm sorry. I pushed right in front of you."

"Miz' Elizabeth," acknowledged Doris with a nod. She gave a faint smile toward Matthew. Did that screen of propriety trickle down to the help?

Doris took their coats and showed them to the parlor where the Caldwells were waiting.

William Caldwell rose as they entered. "How lovely of you young ladies to come. I trust you had an uneventful ride."

"Yes, thank you for sending the car," said Elizabeth.

He turned to his wife, who was sitting by a stone fireplace. "Virginia, I'm sure you remember Andrew's wife, Elizabeth, and Mrs. Thomas, who saw you through your illness."

Virginia Caldwell smiled. She looked at the children as if they were foreign beings.

"I'm afraid Mrs. Caldwell has had a bit of a set-back. Dr. Hawthorne thinks she has had a shock, which has affected her speech and left her weak."

"Mr. Caldwell, I am so sorry," said Elizabeth. "When did this happen?"

"Last week."

"We have seen Dr. Hawthorn. He should have informed us. We wouldn't have come if we had known Mrs. Caldwell is not feeling well."

The gentleman took his wife's hand. "It wasn't the doctor's place. We would have been disappointed if you didn't come to see us. Isn't that right, Virginia?"

She nodded. Carolyn took Annie by the hand and walked to Virginia. She was still the upright, attractive lady of the manor with lovely auburn hair and green eyes. But they were not the sparkling eyes Carolyn remembered. "Mrs. Caldwell, it is good to see you. This is Asa's and my daughter, Ann Catherine. Do you remember Andrew's friend, Asa?"

Virginia hesitated before giving a slow nod. Tears came to her eyes, and she kissed Carolyn's hand.

Elizabeth stood back. Carolyn was so easy and well-received in this house it caused her to feel awkward. She held Matthew's hand in a tight grip so that he couldn't start examining the parlor or worse yet break something. There was an ornamental vase filled with mums just waiting for a little hand to knock it over. The andirons by the fireplace were too inviting as were the books lining a bookcase.

William Caldwell left his wife's side and came to Elizabeth. "Bring Matthew to see his grandmother," he encouraged.

Elizabeth was visibly moved. "Do you think we will upset her?"

He spoke in a confidential tone. "I believe it will be good for her. Elizabeth, I must tell you, Virginia said she was sorry not to be as open as she should have been in July when you and Andrew brought Matthew. She said she should have told you she was pleased Andrew chose you. Even though Matthew is not our flesh and blood grandson, we accept him as ours. It should have all been said at that time. Now, she may never be able to tell you herself."

Elizabeth was choked with emotion as she followed William to where Virginia sat.

Carolyn stepped aside.

She addressed her in a quiet tone. "Hello, Mrs. Caldwell. It's Andrew's wife, Elizabeth."

Virginia smiled and patted Elizabeth's face.

"And, here's Matthew. Matthew can you shake hands?"

Matthew tentatively offered his small hand and let Virginia hold it in hers. She looked up at

Elizabeth as if wanting to say something but no words came.

William Caldwell stepped forward. "Now, let me get introduced to these little ones." He stood with finger to his lips looking at the two toddlers, who held vague expressions. "It isn't difficult to know who belongs to whom or is it whom belongs to who?"

They all chuckled, pleased for the levity after tense moments.

"I do believe Matthew has grown, Elizabeth," was his observation. He rubbed his hands together. "We will be having lunch in a few minutes. The children can eat with us, or Doris can take them to the kitchen for feeding."

Elizabeth looked at Carolyn and they gave an agreeable nod. "If we're free from the children, it will give us time to catch up on news," said Carolyn.

Doris brought the wheelchair to the parlor when lunch was announced.

William Caldwell pointed to the wheelchair. "You see, Mrs. Thomas, this was a good invest-ment."

Carolyn grinned when she saw the wooden high-backed chair wheeled into the room. James Anderson had been the one who had brought the wheelchair from the train station. Carolyn credited it to helping Virginia get well.

William Caldwell helped his wife to her feet while Doris steadied the chair.

81

Millie Curtis

"We haven't had to hire a nurse as of yet." A wan smile gave way to the fact that he hoped they wouldn't have to.

The children eagerly went with Doris when she promised them cookies.

At the dining room table sat William Caldwell, Carolyn and Elizabeth, with Virginia's wheelchair placed next to her husband.

"I expect Emily to join us. Ruth and Will had other plans for today."

"Did they know we were coming?" asked Elizabeth.

"They were informed. Emily was quite enthused. She said she hadn't had time to get acquainted with her new sister-in-law, and she had news for Mrs. Thomas."

"Will, on the other hand, gets wrapped up in farm affairs and sometimes forgets. He is so much different from Andrew, one wouldn't know they are brothers."

"Is Ruth away?" asked Elizabeth.

"Ah, Ruth." He sighed. "One is never quite sure with Ruth."

Elizabeth and Carolyn exchanged a knowing glance.

Ollie had prepared roast pork, scalloped potatoes, carrots and apple pie for their lunch.

Carolyn leaned toward Elizabeth. "I believe we will have soup for supper."

Mr. Caldwell was serving the roast when Emily appeared. "I apologize for being late, but I had to finish a task."

"There are no excuses, Emily," said her father-in-law. "You may take your seat." The man believed in lunch at noon and dinner at six.

"Elizabeth and Carolyn, I am delighted to see you," she greeted them as she took her seat across from them at the table.

Was this a new Emily, thought a surprised Carolyn. She had always been so quiet, demure and insecure. The Emily she remembered would have wilted with the elder Caldwell's reprimand, but Emily had been unruffled.

Once the plates were filled, William Caldwell cut Virginia's meat while addressing Elizabeth. "Tell us about Andrew. We haven't had any word from him since you both came for that two-day visit in July."

Elizabeth didn't apologize. "One of the reasons for our trip back to Clarke County is to tell you that Andrew and Asa have been shipped off to Europe."

"What! Why weren't we told?"

The news didn't seem to register with Virginia, who was intent on manipulating her utensils with one hand.

"Andrew didn't want to worry you. They had little time to prepare."

"How insensitive! He should have told us."

"Father Caldwell, I'm sure Andrew had your best interests at heart," enjoined Emily.

"We haven't had any word from either of them," said Carolyn. "But, Catherine Burke, who came with us, received a letter from her husband, yesterday. He wrote that Asa and Andrew are in charge of setting up division headquarters in a town in northeastern France. Catherine's husband is a doctor who has offered his services."

William Caldwell contemplated the information. "Most of the fighting is in the western and southern parts of Europe as I understand it, so I guess they are safe," said the concerned father.

"I shall have to tell James Anderson," said Emily. "The other day he was giving Will some insight about a horse, and I heard him ask if the war had affected Andrew. You do remember James, Carolyn?"

"Of course." How could she forget him? To change the subject, Carolyn said to Emily. "Mr. Caldwell says you have news for me."

"I do. You were so wise to direct me into teaching our farm help, I have taught some of the adults how to read and enough about math to take care of what little income they get. Best of all, one of my pupils will be going to the normal school in Harrisonburg to become a teacher."

"Anyone I know?" asked Carolyn.

"One of the Coleman girls."

Carolyn's jaw dropped. "That isn't possible. That hopeless family?"

"Exactly. She showed promise, and I wasn't wrong."

"Where is the money coming from?"

"A scholarship and a generous donation from Father Caldwell."

William Caldwell cleared his throat.

"Wonderful," said Carolyn.

"Tell us about the children," encouraged Emily. "I hope you brought them."

"We did," said Elizabeth. "Ollie and Doris are feeding them lunch in the kitchen so we could have some time to visit."

"Good, I'll go down with you once lunch is done."

"I hope Matthew isn't tearing the kitchen apart. He's more inquisitive than I can keep up with sometimes."

"Let's have our pie and then you young ladies can go retrieve your offspring," suggested William.

In the kitchen, they found Ollie and Doris singing and dancing around with Annie and Matthew in their arms.

"Miz' Carolyn!" exclaimed Ollie when she spotted them. She set Annie on the floor and ran to give Carolyn a big hug.

"Ollie, how good to see you."

Annie toddled over and clung to Carolyn's skirt. She patted her daughter on the head. "Hi, sweetheart."

"We have bin' havin' the best time with these two. Why don' you move back here so's we can watch them grow up?"

"There's a big world out there, Ollie. I want to see it."

Matthew had warmed to Emily and they were playing Peas, Porridge Hot. "Why not, Elizabeth?" asked Emily.

"Why not what?"

"Why not move here, at least while Andrew is in the war? His rooms sit idle upstairs. It would be good for all of us. Maybe it would put some life into this place."

"What about it, Elizabeth?" asked Carolyn.

"I'm satisfied in the city." Although she was not pleased to be living with her parents.

"I think we done filled them up on cookies and tired them out," said Doris. "I spect' they's gonna' sleep all the way back to Berryville."

"Thank you for being so good to us by taking care of them," said Elizabeth. "Stuart said he would bring the car around at two, so we'd better get going."

At two-fifteen, they said their goodbyes and climbed into the back seat of the Packard.

As predicted, Annie and Matthew fell fast asleep.

On the way back to Berryville, Carolyn turned to Elizabeth. "Maybe you should give some thought to moving back here until Andrew returns."

"Why should I want to do that? You're more at home at Red Gate than I am," Elizabeth replied. "In case you didn't notice, Ruth and Will not showing up was a clear snub, and who knows what is happening with Andrew's mother? No thank you, Carolyn, I'll struggle with living with my parents. At least I know what to expect."

"Sorry I mentioned it," came Carolyn's sheepish reply.

Chapter 9

Thaddeus Hawthorne drove Catherine the two blocks to the closed hat shop. "I'll see you up to the apartment," he offered.

Before they could get out of the Model T, Carolyn came bursting out the front door and down the short set of steps.

She was jubilant. "I've been watching for you! We're so happy you're back." She yanked open the door and grabbed Catherine's small satchel out of her hands. She ducked her head inside the auto. "Any special instructions, Dr. Hawthorne?"

"Mrs. Burke has her orders," he replied with a half-smile. "Are you sure you don't want to stay in town? I can use a good nurse."

Carolyn laughed. "I'll keep it in mind." She held the door open as Catherine stepped out.

"I'm on my way to a house call. Mrs. Hawthorne wanted me to remind you that she is expecting you young ladies to dine with her at the Battletown Inn on Saturday evening."

"We are looking forward to it," responded Catherine. "Thank you for all you've done."

He put the car into gear and rattled away.

"Let's hurry in before Lavinia spots us," said Catherine. "I don't think I'm up to her."

But, they were too late.

"Halloo." She waved her handkerchief as she came waddling across the street.

Carolyn groaned.

"Hello, Mrs. Talley," said Catherine.

"Elizabeth told me you were ill. It's good to see you recovered. I just wanted to say how pleased I am to see you back in town." Then as an after-thought, "You, too, Carolyn."

The woman didn't skip a beat. "Now Catherine, I trust your ailment isn't catching."

"The doctor assured me it isn't. Although, one can never be too careful."

"Oh," she twittered and took a step back.

"Jeremy would like to put an item in the *Courier* about your visit."

"Mrs. Talley, we are planning on returning to Washington the day after tomorrow," informed Carolyn. "As the paper doesn't come out until next week, it would be old news."

Lavinia shot a mind your own business look at Carolyn. "Elizabeth informed me your men have gone off to war."

Catherine felt testy. "Perhaps that would make headlines: *Three Young Women On Their Own After Shipping Their Husbands Off To War.*"

Lavinia chuckled. "It's good to see you haven't lost your sense of humor."

"Mrs. Talley, you will have to excuse us. I am quite tired," said Catherine.

"Yes dear, I'm sure you are." She hesitated before asking, with a slight cock of her head, "Was it a female problem?"

"You understand how those things are. Now, I really must go inside." Catherine turned on her heel and went toward the stoop with Carolyn close behind, leaving Lavinia standing on the sidewalk.

Unabashed, Lavinia turned and waddled back home.

Mounting the stairs to the apartment, Carolyn said, "That woman is so irritating. For a moment, I thought you might tell her about your misfortune."

"Why would I do that? It doesn't need to be splashed in the paper."

Carolyn was thoughtful. "It's good we're leaving on Sunday."

"What did you think about Dr. Hawthorne offering you a position?"

"I don't think he was serious. It was just something nice to say."

Elizabeth was playing with the children when they came into the apartment.

"It took you long enough. I saw Mrs. Talley toddle across the street. I don't have to ask what she wanted. How are you feeling, Catherine?"

"Tired. Better."

"Good. I'll get some graham crackers for Annie and Matthew. I made hot cocoa. Would you both like to have a cup?"

Carolyn replied, "It will be welcome. I'll help with the little ones while Catherine takes a few minutes to settle in. Then we can enjoy cocoa in the living room." She glanced at Elizabeth, "We'll fill Catherine in about our trip over to Red Gate Farm."

"I'll be all ears," said Catherine as she headed toward the bedroom.

An hour later they sat sipping cocoa; Catherine was lounging on the flowered chintz sofa, Carolyn and Elizabeth were sitting in the matching chairs.

"I don't know why I left this living room set. I've always been fond of it," Catherine said as she ran a hand over the satiny material.

"I'm glad you did. I can't say it is that comfortable to sleep on." Elizabeth propped her feet on top of a small hassock. "If the hat shop sells, I may decide to keep the set...unless you want it back, Catherine."

Catherine shook her head.

Annie and Matthew were playing on the floor with toys the Hawthorne children had let them borrow.

Carolyn looked over at Elizabeth. "They won't want to give them back, you know."

"We'll confront that problem when it happens. The toys keep them out from under our feet."

Catherine smiled down at the children with a wistful look. "Tell me about your trip to see Andrew's parents."

Carolyn was eager to give the story. "Mr. and Mrs. Caldwell seemed pleased we came, although she is not doing well. Dr. Hawthorne thinks she had a shock which has affected her ability to speak. She is also weak and they use a wheelchair for her."

"Did she know you?"

"I'm sure she did, and also Elizabeth. She seemed a bit confused with the children."

"What does the doctor expect?"

"I thought Mr. Caldwell a bit vague on that subject, didn't you, Carolyn?" asked Elizabeth.

"What could he say in front of his wife? She understands what is said. I believe it is a case of regaining what was lost or going into a slow decline."

"I am sorry to hear that. Let's talk about what was good about the visit," encouraged Catherine.

It was Elizabeth's turn. "For Carolyn, it was wonderful. Everyone welcomed her with open arms. We ate in the lovely dining room with its lace curtains and crystal chandelier. Andrew's sister-in-law, Emily, was the only one who joined us. Will and Ruth made other plans, most likely because they don't approve of me."

Catherine shifted her position to lean on an arm of the sofa. "Why should that bother you? They're both pains in the neck."

"Well said," agreed Carolyn. "Emily, on the other hand, was delightful. I couldn't believe the change in her. One of the Coleman girls she taught is going on to become a teacher. Isn't that hard to believe?"

"Pat yourself on the back, Carolyn. You helped her get off the hooch."

91

Elizabeth's eyes opened wide. "You mean she had a drinking problem?"

"Catherine! You shouldn't have said that," admonished Carolyn.

"It's the truth. If it hadn't been for the time you spent over at Red Gate, she may still be in a rut." Catherine looked squarely at Elizabeth. "I don't know how Andrew turned out so well. It's common knowledge that his sister is a gadfly and his brother is pomposity personified. I'm tired of your feeling inferior as Andrew's wife. You've got spirit, show some of it."

Elizabeth was taken aback by Catherine's chastisement but only for a moment. "Thank you, Catherine. I think that's the nicest thing you've ever said to me."

One after the other they started to laugh, loud belly laughs until tears rolled down their cheeks: tears of loss, tears of resentment, tears of release.

Matthew and Annie stopped their play. Confused and upset, they ran to their mothers. What was wrong? Mommies don't cry.

**

In the afternoon, Catherine rested in the bedroom. Elizabeth went down to the hat shop, as she hadn't even peeked inside it since they'd arrived, and Carolyn put the toddlers down for a nap. She was hanging up wet diapers in the living room when she heard the grating of the handle in the entry door.

She hurried down the stairs before another turning woke the children. Carolyn opened the door with chagrin. "James!"

He doffed his cap. "Hello, Carolyn. I heard you were in town." His engaging smile always made her weak in the knees. As tall and handsome as ever, she stood breathless.

"Aren't you going to invite me in?"

"Of course. You left me speechless, I am so surprised to see you. Come in."

"You look lovely. I would say being a wife and mother agrees with you."

She smoothed her apron, tidied her hair and felt her face turn a delicate pink.

"Don't embarrass me, James. I know how I look. Can you come upstairs for a cup of tea?"

He took her hand and kissed it. "I have a few minutes."

They started up the wide staircase side by side.

She felt her heart pounding and determined to stay as nonchalant as she could.

"We'll sit in the kitchen. The children are asleep, and I have diapers hanging in the living room."

He smiled as he took a seat at the table. "How long will you be here?"

"We plan on leaving Sunday."

"So soon?"

"We only came for the week."

"I understand Andrew's wife is with you."

"Yes. Catherine Burke, also."

93

Carolyn brushed off the table with her apron. "The water is already hot for tea. We have some oatmeal cookies. Would you care for one?"

He watched as she moved around the small kitchen. "Tea will be fine."

Carolyn poured the tea before sitting opposite James.

"You don't know how much I've missed you," he said. "Do you remember the first time we met when I drove you to Red Gate Farm?"

"How could I forget?" She chuckled. "You scared me out of my wits, you were so self-assured."

"I still am. Carolyn, I haven't regretted my decision to marry Amanda. When her father died, he left the estate in both our names."

"How is Amanda?"

"She's so high-strung, she'll probably have apoplexy like her father did."

Carolyn grimaced. "I know you married her for money, but I never expected you to be so callous."

He gave a half-smile. "I'm being realistic. She is well aware of our arrangement, so we live together and put on a good show."

"Then she's as insensitive as you are. I suppose it isn't more than I expected. Is the place doing well?"

"As I've told you before, I am the best horse breeder in this area and we are producing excellent lines. I spend much of my time with bookwork and in the stables."

"I'm glad you are satisfied. I'm happy I left, James. Unfortunately, Asa has been shipped over to Europe, but I'm hoping it will only be for six months."

"How can you calculate a war?"

"Hopefulness. Would you like to see our daughter? We can sneak in and take a peek. Matthew is napping beside her."

"Is that the child Andrew adopted? I heard about that, too."

She gave a disgusted look. "I'm sure you did. I trust it was not in a snide way."

He didn't answer. "I do need to be on my way. Let's go see your little one."

They tiptoed into the dining room. James stood with cap in hand as he admired the sleeping pair.

They left as quietly as they had entered.

On their way down the stairs, James said, "She is beautiful, Carolyn. She favors you with her coloring, that cute little nose and pouty mouth."

"Asa loves her dearly. I pray we will not be separated for long."

He stood with her at the bottom of the stairs. "You are still in love?"

"He is a good man," was her reply.

James touched the tip of her nose. "We had some memorable times together. Remember, you are still my true love. Goodbye, Carolyn." Before going out the door, he kissed her forehead leaving her dumbstruck!

Elizabeth came into the foyer from the adjoining hat shop. "Carolyn, it's you. I thought I heard voices. Are you all right?"

"Numb. I just said goodbye to James Anderson."

"Isn't he the one you said used to work for the Caldwells?"

"The same. He was my ally when I cared for Mrs. Caldwell. I had a big crush on him."

Elizabeth contemplated her friend. "Are you sure it was only a passing infatuation?"

Carolyn offered a weak smile. "Let's go up and get supper started."

Chapter 10

Saturday morning arrived with a bright November sun streaming in the bedroom window. Catherine poked Carolyn. "It's eight o'clock and I don't hear the children."

Carolyn woke up hazy. "What did you say?"

"I said, it's eight o'clock and I don't hear a sound, I wonder if the children are all right."

Carolyn hopped out of bed with alarm. "I haven't slept that late in two years."

She hurried out of the bedroom and opened the door to where the little ones slept. There they were sitting on the bedroom floor in their nightclothes with toys strewn about and pillows pulled off the small bed they shared.

Matthew looked up. "Ball," he said and threw a ball in Carolyn's direction.

Annie got to her feet. "Ma-ma."

Carolyn picked her up and took Matthew's hand.

Catherine met her in the hallway. "What's going on? Where is Elizabeth?"

"I don't know, I just got here. Check the living room."

They pushed aside the line of drying diapers and there was Elizabeth, asleep on the chintz sofa.

Catherine gave her a gentle shake. "Wake up."

"Ooh," she groaned. "I've been awake most of the night."

Carolyn was to the point. "I hope you're not sick."

Elizabeth sat up and Matthew climbed up to sit on her lap. She kissed his cheek. "No, I'm not sick. My mind didn't want to settle down. I'm worried about Andrew, and I dread going back to listen to my mother. Look at my hands. They're red and chapped from washing those diapers."

Carolyn had no sympathy. "So are mine. Don't you wash them at home?"

"Certainly not. Opal washes them in the copper washing machine."

"How dreadful," came Carolyn's breezy remark. "You both get dressed while I cook up oatmeal for breakfast. These two aren't going to be in good humor too much longer."

The children were fed and dressed and put back in the jumbled playroom. "I'll clean this up later," said Carolyn. "They'll only mess it up again."

The three women sat at the kitchen table having breakfast.

"Elizabeth, you can't afford to lose sleep over worry," said Carolyn.

"That's easier said than done. What do you suggest?"

"I think you should do some serious think-ing about staying at Red Gate Farm until Andrew returns. That would solve the problem of your mother."

"Did the Caldwells invite you to stay?" asked Catherine.

"No," answered Elizabeth. "That was Emily's idea."

"Maybe you should think about it."

"I already have and the answer is no."

Catherine smiled. "That sounds final to me."

Elizabeth stirred her coffee with a spoon. "I'll tell you something else I've been thinking about."

Carolyn perked up. "What's that?"

"I read about a program called the "Hello Girls". They're being hired by the U.S. Army to handle communications in France."

"Elizabeth! That's as crazy as Carolyn wanting to become an army nurse," came Catherine's reprimand.

"I still think I should go over as a nurse."

Catherine shook her head. "I don't believe what I am hearing. Unless you have forgotten, you have children to care for. What would become of them? No, if any of us were free to help it would be me. The Red Cross is desperate for volunteers."

Two heads snapped to attention. "Catherine. Have you been considering that?"

"I did a lot of thinking while I endured those long hours at the Hawthorne House. I can close up the house in Georgetown for six months."

Carolyn was annoyed. "That wouldn't be fair if you got to go and we didn't."

"Life is never fair, Carolyn. I'm sure the French women are eager to help and that bothers me. Many of them have lost their men. My mind plays tricks on what could transpire between the French women and the American men."

"Don't you trust Patrick?" asked Elizabeth.

"Let's say that the less temptation thrown in any man's way, the better. They are thousands of miles away, in a strange land, tired and lonely."

Looks of consternation appeared on the faces of Carolyn and Elizabeth as if they had been struck.

"You did too much thinking, Catherine. But, I've got an idea," gushed Carolyn.

Catherine gave a deep sigh. "I can hardly wait to hear this one."

"Let's all go and take Mattie with us. "She can watch the children. I can work in a hospital, Catherine can volunteer with the Red Cross and Elizabeth can look into this Hello Girl business."

The three glanced at each other. It was something to think about.

**

That evening, they left Annie and Matthew in the care of the Hawthorne twins while they joined Grace Hawthorne at the Battletown Inn for dinner. The Inn was located in the hotel and considered one of the finest places to eat in the area. They sat at a square oak table covered with a white tablecloth. A candle in the middle of the table sent up fine tendrils of gray smoke. A fireplace warmed the interior of the comfortable room with its high ceiling. They ordered tea and smothered chicken, a specialty of the Inn.

"I am so pleased you could join me before you leave tomorrow," said Grace. "Elizabeth, have you had any interested parties to buy the shop?"

"No. I wish it would sell. There is no mortgage, but there are still the taxes to pay. It looks the same as when I left it in June." She gave a slight chuckle. "Perhaps a bit more dust."

They offered sympathetic smiles.

"Tell me about your husbands. I know Catherine received a letter from Dr. Burke. Have either of you had any word?"

"We expect there are letters awaiting our return. According to Patrick's letter, Asa and Andrew are in charge of setting up headquarters for their division," answered Carolyn. "I can't imagine they have a moment to themselves."

"They are together and that gives us solace," said Elizabeth. "You know, the American Expeditionary forces are only there to lend aid. We are hoping that they will return in six months. I guess that is five months now that they left a month ago."

"But, you can't be sure of that, can you?" asked Grace.

"We remain hopeful," said Catherine.

Grace's smile was benevolent. "Of course you should. Have any of you thought about moving back here?"

101

Catherine answered for all three. "I believe we are settled."

The waiter brought the main dish. They spread linen napkins on their laps and lapsed into silence as they began to eat.

"Elizabeth, would you mind lifting that tea cozy and feel if the pot is still warm?" asked Catherine. "I could use another cup."

"I believe we can all use a fresh cup," said Grace, who signaled the waiter to bring another pot of tea. "What will you girls do on your return?"

Catherine gave Carolyn a wary eye, afraid she was going to tell Grace about what they had discussed that morning.

Carolyn caught the cautionary look and cleared her throat. "There is always something to keep us busy. We may look into volunteer work to help in the war effort."

Grace was not one to carry tales, but one accidental slip about going to Europe to help the troops and it would be splashed all over the *Courier.*

"Well, I do wish you still lived here. It was such a joy to visit the hat shop and see all the lovely hats, gloves and jewelry." She turned to Carolyn. "And, I must tell you that Thaddeus misses you in the office."

Carolyn smiled, "It's kind of you to say."

"It is the truth."

The waiter came by the table with a dessert tray. "Would you ladies care for dessert? We have bread pudding, apple cobbler and Martha Washington cake."

Catherine waved away the temptation.

"I am much too full," said the delicate Elizabeth.

But characteristic of Carolyn, she jumped at the chance to have a piece of Martha Washington cake.

"Perhaps, a tiny dish of bread pudding," said Grace, bringing a smile to Catherine's face.

Grace was slim as a willow branch and a much better candidate for the rich cake loaded with butter, eggs, and spices and lavishly frosted with a heavy creamy frosting.

When dinner was over they returned to the Hawthornes', bundled up the children and started out. The street lights did a poor job of lighting the way. The small band walked the familiar street past Irene Butler's dress shop, the barber shop, crossed Church Street, and mounted the short set of steps to the stoop.

There was much to do before taking the noon train back to Washington the next day.

Chapter 11

Herbert Marks, handlebar mustache, canvas duster and wool driving cap, took a proud stand as he opened the back door of the 1913 Cadillac Grand 'Torpedo' Touring Car for the young ladies to enter.

The automobile was impressive: body of forest green, black spoke wheels rimmed in white, fenders, black leather padded seats, chrome trim, black leather top that could be folded down in summer, and a shiny black running board, which Herbert promptly dusted off after the women and children were settled. The car was cramped so the children sat on their mothers' laps.

He had piled their luggage in the front seat and on the floor board. Catherine had to hold one of Elizabeth's satchels as hers was the only free lap. The satchel wouldn't fit in front, no matter how many mild oaths Herbert swore under his breath.

"Usually only have two or three riders and they each bring one case," he complained.

"Elizabeth, you are going to have to learn to drag less paraphernalia," advised Catherine.

She sighed, "I know."

The "For Sale" sign still hung in the window of the hat shop. Catherine took a long look. "How could it be that I was born and raised here, ran the hat shop, and, in only two years, it seems like another world?"

"I only owned the place for a year and I feel the same way," agreed Elizabeth. "You have your shop in Georgetown, perhaps that's why you don't mind not owning this millinery."

"Patrick was wise to realize what a transition moving to Georgetown would be for me. He encouraged me to set up that shop. Elizabeth, I hope this one sells so you don't have to think about it. You can always rent out the apartment."

"I'd just like to be rid of the whole place."

Herbert took his seat behind the leather-wrapped steering wheel. He craned his long stork-like neck. "You ladies ready for the chug up the mountain?"

"We can't miss this train, I trust we'll be on time." Catherine was not one to be late.

"Why, Miz' Catherine, Are you sayin' I ain't dependable?"

"No, Mr. Marks. You have always been dependable. We just couldn't depend on you being on time," she replied.

He let out a loud guffaw. "You ladies are goin' to have to come more often. Sure brightens up the place."

As the auto pulled away, Lavinia Talley stood in her doorway and waved a handkerchief as they left Berryville behind.

The train was waiting when they reached the small Bluemont station. Carolyn collected money and went inside to buy three tickets. As long as the children sat on their mothers' laps, they rode without charge.

Elizabeth and Catherine took the children into the train car to secure favorable seats. There were few passengers boarding, but when the train made its way off the mountain and stopped at the hamlets and towns in between, the car would be full before they reached Alexandria. They chose seats facing each other so the women could converse.

Elizabeth sat her satchel on the seat beside her. She opened the latch and pulled out Matthew's crib blanket. It was becoming tattered but she overlooked its appearance. The blanket had come with him when she and Andrew picked him up at the orphanage. It never failed to be the calming influence when he was distressful.

"Isn't it time to wean him away from that before it falls apart?" asked Catherine.

"No. He can carry it around when he goes to school if he wants to. As long as it keeps him comforted, I'll not interfere."

Catherine smiled. "I'd probably feel the same way."

"Ma-ma," exclaimed Annie when she saw her mother making her way down the aisle.

"Hi sweetheart." She edged in next to Catherine and transferred Annie to her lap. "This might work out quite well," she observed. "We have three laps and only two children."

"We should switch seats before the train gets underway." Catherine rose so Carolyn could sit by the window.

While making the awkward switch, the train whistle blew and the railcar lurched forward causing Catherine to plop into her seat.

Elizabeth, who was tying Matthew's shoe-lace, turned her head with an abrupt twist. "Are you all right, Catherine? Do you think this jostling is going to bother you?" She looked over at Carolyn. "Perhaps we should have stayed a couple more days."

Catherine leaned forward and answered in a confidential tone. "No. My body feels like it is just experiencing that monthly curse all we women have to endure."

Elizabeth was embarrassed. "Catherine! I hope no one heard that."

"How could they? The next passengers are three seats ahead and who can hear anything over the rattle of this train?" The tone of her voice changed. "I will be honest with you. Although, I have been able to resolve this loss, if I had carried the baby further along, I'm not sure I could have endured it."

Carolyn chimed in. "Let's be glad that is all behind us. We have the future to think about."

It was three-fifteen in the afternoon when they arrived at the Alexandria station. The children and Catherine had awakened when the train slowed its pace.

"You're all groggy," observed Carolyn. "I can't believe you slept the whole way."

Catherine rubbed her eyes and slowly came to life. "I can't either. Did we make all those stops along the way?"

Elizabeth grinned. "We did. Carolyn and I didn't even get off the train in Leesburg because we didn't want to wake any of you sleepyheads."

Catherine looked at the two little ones. Ann Catherine was yawning and Matthew was scratching his blonde head. "We were good children for our mommies, weren't we?"

They gave blank stares.

"Elizabeth, why don't you call your father and see if he will come pick us up? He goes right past our trolley stop," Carolyn suggested.

"Do you think we can all fit into that Tin Lizzy?"

"If he doesn't bring your mother, we can," Carolyn remarked.

"I can't very well ask him to leave Mother home if she wants to come."

They were collecting their things.

"Why not?" asked Carolyn. "He just has to tell her that he needs to give us all a ride."

"In the first place, it would be impolite and, in the second place, I will hear repercussions from my mother."

Catherine didn't have time for their petty dispute. "Carolyn, once the porter places our luggage on the platform, if you will carry my suitcase, I'll carry Elizabeth's flowered satchel. It's much lighter."

Carolyn looked up from what she was doing. "You take Annie's hand because I can't carry both suitcases and hold onto her. Elizabeth, I don't know why you had to pack so much stuff."

"You were happy enough to have the extra diapers," Elizabeth retorted.

"Oh, it's good to be back home," came Catherine's tongue-in-cheek statement. "Come with your Auntie Catherine, children, and I'll buy you each a lollipop."

The two disgruntled mothers stopped wrestling with their cumbersome belongings and shot wary looks at Catherine.

"They're going to get sticky," said Elizabeth.

"I hope so," answered Catherine and started down the aisle with two toddlers in tow.

That evening Catherine was worn out when she reached her home in Georgetown. The quiet house held no warmth when she entered. She snapped on a light in the foyer, unpinned her hat and left her suitcase on the floor. She was too tired to do anything but drink a glass of water before she dragged herself upstairs to the lonesome bedroom.

Both Elizabeth and Carolyn had offered to see her home but she refused. She preferred to be alone. The week had been draining, a poignant reminder of the losses she'd suffered.

When Patrick made the decision to help in the war, Catherine had pinned her hopes on bringing a new life into the world. The excitement and anticipation would be enough to carry her through until he came back. Now those hopes were dashed.

The nagging thought that he might not return could not be pushed from her mind causing her anguish beyond words.

Her mind worked overtime until she fell into an exhausted sleep.

Chapter 12

Carolyn telephoned before eight o'clock the next morning.

"Catherine. It's good to hear your voice. I should have called last evening, but by the time I got a chance to call it was late, and I didn't want to disturb you if you were asleep. I have a letter from Asa!"

Catherine was half-awake. "I'm glad you didn't call. I went straight to bed." With a start, Carolyn's words sunk in. "Asa! What does he have to say?"

"I'd rather not read it over the phone."

"I understand. I'll be here, why don't you bring Ann Catherine over. You can read Asa's letter and I'll tell you what is milling around in my tired mind."

"Annie just finished her breakfast. We'll come over as soon as I get her ready."

Catherine replaced the receiver with an unfamiliar sense of relief. Perhaps what she was considering wasn't as far afield as she had thought.

Carolyn arrived as bright and eager as ever. She came in the front door as Mattie came in the back.

Catherine was picking up the suitcase she'd left in the foyer the night before. "My goodness, three of my favorite people all at the same time."

"Miz' Catherine. I came to check on the house."

Annie ran to the large woman and threw her arms around her legs.

Mattie swooped her up in her strong arms and planted a kiss on her cheek causing Annie to giggle with glee. "Look at you, chile'. Miz' Mattie ain't seen you fer a spell and you done sprouted like a mushroom." She set the child on the floor. "How you been Miz' Catherine? Was it a good trip?"

"It was a trip like one I had never taken before. While you're here, would you mind putting the kettle over for tea?"

"How 'bout I put the kettle over and take little Miz' Annie outdoors to play? Jacob's out in the back dressin' up the yard. I know he'd like to see her."

Carolyn nodded her agreement.

"How is Jacob?" asked Catherine. "I'll be writing a letter to Patrick and he will want to know if you and Jacob are well."

"He be fine. You know how husbands can worry their wives sometimes, but I guess that's the way life is."

Out to the kitchen they went, hand in hand, with Ann Catherine jabbering away in gibberish.

Carolyn looked at Catherine. "I wonder if she is ever going to talk so she can be understood. Matthew is putting words together."

"Matthew is three months older. I have a feeling once our Ann Catherine starts to talk, we'll wish she didn't have so much to say. Let's go have tea. I'm dying to hear what Asa has written."

They sat at the familiar kitchen table.

My dear Carolyn,

This will be short as private time is scarce.

Andrew and I are still in the midst of supervising the setting up of headquarters. I'm sure Patrick has sent a letter with that information.

The rain has been relentless causing the horses and mules to get bogged down in mud trying to get supplies up here from Brest, a seaport some miles south of us.

The French are training us in trench warfare, which is new to us. As soon as the gas masks arrive, we will all be trained in the use of those.

The town is quaint with a large square for gatherings and celebrations. I believe there are more soldiers than townspeople, but they are welcoming. I wish I spoke French

I cannot express how much I miss you and our beautiful little Annie. I fear she will forget me.

I must close. Know that I love you with all my being.

Your faithful husband,
Asa

Carolyn folded the letter with care and put it into her sweater pocket. They sat transfixed before Catherine spoke, "When did he write the letter?"

"It isn't dated."

Again they sat in quiet contemplation until Catherine proposed, "How would you like to spend Christmas in France?"

For once Carolyn was struck wordless. Her recovery was quick. "Did I hear you right?"

"I did a lot of thinking while I was at the Hawthorne House. I am still concerned that Patrick won't come back. I have nothing holding me here but this house. I would rather spend some moments of bliss if I am to be left a widow."

Carolyn hit her fist on the table. "Do you remember how you told Elizabeth you didn't want to hear her put herself down? Well, I don't want to hear any more about Patrick not coming home. It's time you put that thought out of your mind. He is coming back!"

Catherine's head snapped up in surprise. "I'll try," came her quiet reply.

"Now, how do you propose we get there?"

"You mean you want to go?"

"Of course I do. Weren't you the one who pooh-poohed my idea of joining the Army Nurse Corps?"

Catherine chuckled. "I guess I did."

"Do you have anything to go with this tea?"

"All I have in the house are those ears of popcorn Mary Lee gave us."

"Let's shuck some kernels and pop them up, I'm hungry."

When Mattie returned with Ann Catherine, she found the two friends sitting at the table eating from an enamel dishpan full of fluffy white popcorn.

She took off Annie's coat and bonnet and pulled a stool to the table and sat her next to her mother.

"Jacob said she's growed a mite since he seen her. I done gots' ta'wash her hands before you give her some of that corn."

"Have some popcorn with us," suggested Catherine.

"No, ma'am. I don't like all that chaffy stuff that gets stuck in yer teeth."

"Mattie, how would you like to go to France for Christmas?" asked Catherine.

The big woman wrinkled her brow. "Miz' Catherine, I think you done addled yer brain."

"No I am perfectly lucid. Miss Carolyn and I are making plans to go. We would like to have you come to watch the children."

"Children? Miz' Elizabeth is goin' too?"

"She doesn't know it, yet, but she will," answered Carolyn as she grabbed another handful of popcorn.

The large colored woman looked at the two women as though they had lost their minds. "Mm, mm, mm." She shook her head. "I don' know what's got into you, Miz' Catherine. I jus' know it ain't likely I'm goin' to no place I don' know nthin' about."

Chapter 13

Two weeks before the Christmas of 1917, three apprehensive young women, a worried colored maid and two awestruck children were standing on a cold dock in a New York harbor waiting to board the HMT Czar. A bone-chilling wind whipped about causing choppy waves that rocked the big boat to and fro.

The ocean liner was overpowering in its size. Two funnels and two masts rose tall into the air. The ship had been part of the Russian-American line, but now belonged to the British. A 'Gem of the Ocean' was how the advertisement read.

Matthew and Ann Catherine stared in amazement. Mattie said a silent prayer and Carolyn, the adventurous one, swallowed hard and asked with mild trepidation, "Do you think we have made a mistake?"

There was no answer. Catherine and Elizabeth seemed to be contemplating what lay ahead.

Then Catherine voiced in a confident manner, "We've paid our fare. People sail on these boats all the time without any problems."

"We didn't tell the men we were coming. What if we get lost at sea?" groaned Elizabeth.

"Lordy! Lordy!" exclaimed Mattie and threw up her hands.

"Let's all calm down. We've planned this well. Patrick knows we are coming. He knows Asa and Andrew will be in Neufchateau, which is only only about five miles away. He will meet us in Brest when we land and has made accommodations for all of us. We must set our eyes on France and being reunited with our husbands."

Carolyn conquered her doubt. "You're right Catherine. I guess I got cold feet when I saw the size of the ship. Speaking of cold, I'm iced through. I wish we were boarding. Our luggage is aboard before we are."

Elizabeth shivered. "If we'd bought first class, as I wanted to, we would already be on ship."

"If you wanted to go first class, you could have," said a miffed Carolyn.

"Don't you two start," cautioned Catherine. "Once we get settled everyone will feel better. Look, they're starting to send our group up the gangplank now."

Carolyn held Annie and Mattie carried Matthew as the tight little band made its way down the wet wooden wharf along with a crowd of passengers. The three women were sensibly dressed in winter coats, warm gloves and snug hats that covered their ears.

Deck hands hurried down to carry the children and escort the trio of attractive young ladies to the main deck of the ship. Mattie was left to struggle her large girth up the gangplank using the guide ropes.

Catherine had purchased the reservations. What Carolyn and Elizabeth didn't know was that Mattie was excluded from riding first class. She was allowed to stay with them in second class as long as they booked rooms in the tail end of the ship where the noise from the engines was the loudest. Otherwise, Mattie would be relegated to a servants' area in the lower part of the liner. Of course Catherine had to pay extra for arranging for her maid, but she was comfortable in her decision. Her friends didn't need to know.

Their staterooms faced each other on either side of a dimly lit and narrow passageway. Once the door opened into the cabin, each room had a porthole that allowed light to enter and afforded a view of the ocean. Cabins could accommodate two, three and four passengers. Catherine had booked the two passenger staterooms for each. That allowed her ample space and she knew Mattie would be more comfortable by herself. Besides, it wouldn't do to share a room with her maid.

The small cabins were equipped with two bunk beds, a settee, a small desk and a compartmented closet. The furnishings weren't lavish but attractive. The purser assured her the second class cabins were as well appointed as the first class. Catherine wondered.

The storm outside had subsided allowing the big boat to settle into a gentle rock. Once the women were situated in their staterooms, Carolyn was ready to explore the ship.

Matthew and Annie were napping and Mattie agreed to keep an eye on them. The three women stood in Catherine's room looking at a map of the ocean liner.

"According to this, our level has the same layout as the upper deck. I believe we are as well off as if we had paid extra for first class passage," surmised Carolyn.

"I'd still like to get up there and look at it," said Elizabeth. "I'm sure it is opulently furnished."

"You just want to get up there to see how the ladies are dressed," said a knowing Catherine.

Elizabeth gave a slight toss of her blonde hair and shrugged a shoulder. "That could be part of it."

"Let's first find the baths and lavatories," suggested Catherine.

"A good idea," the others agreed.

After freshening up in the lavatory and using the map as a guide, they found the ladies saloon, the writing room, the dining room and the gentlemen's smoking room.

The dining room, which accommodated one hundred guests at a sitting, was finished with polished oak. Table settings of silver were in place, along with linen napkins folded in such a way they gave the appearance of a line of teepees on the long tables.

The writing room was a quiet place with oriental carpets and cherry tables with matching chairs placed to allow privacy.

The three explorers took seats on leather benches in the ladies saloon. They admired the flowered carpet, iconic columns, lavish velvet drapes and plush chairs. A corner of the stately room held reading material, a piano and phonograph.

"I believe we could entertain the children in here. There's plenty of room for them to stretch and play," observed Carolyn.

Elizabeth sighed. "I'm dreading these nine days with Matthew. He's got more energy than I have. Look at that map again, Carolyn. There might be a play area for children and their nannies."

"Mattie will keep him in tow," said Catherine. "You know, she's scared to death about this trip. Having the children to watch will keep her busy. She told me the only reason she agreed to come was because 'you ladies needs some time with yer men'. She also told me that I had no business coming by myself."

"Mattie has such a good heart," said Elizabeth. "We need to do something special for her when we return."

"You two can decide on that when the time comes," advised Catherine. "I'm going back to my stateroom and get some rest before it's time for dinner. What time is that on the schedule?"

"Six o'clock," answered Carolyn. "We should all get some rest."

**

After three days at sea, the women felt comfortable on the ship. They looked forward to the meals in the large dining room and entertainment in the saloon in the evenings. Hours of reading or joining in singing along with the piano player afforded them relaxation that soothed any cares they did their best to conceal.

Mattie and the children were relegated to a small dining room near their staterooms. She told Catherine she had the company of another maid who was caring for an infant of a well-to-do couple. They stayed in the plushest cabin on the other end of the ocean liner and left the baby with the maid a few doors from Mattie's room. According to Mattie, the maid told her the couple wanted to have the baby with them only when it was important to look like doting parents. Otherwise, the baby remained with the maid.

While the trio of young ladies spent time in the lounge, Mattie and her like companion watched over their sleeping charges while playing checkers.

The children also settled into the rhythm of the boat. They were always eager to spend time with their mothers either strolling the promenade deck or watching a shuffleboard match. The sea air acted as a panacea: calming, carefree, peaceful.

For Catherine, it had been six weeks since she had lost her baby. It had taken that long for a healthy glow to return to her cheeks and the sadness to leave. She was going to be reunited with Patrick and she was happy. Had it only been two and a half months since he had left Washington? It seemed forever.

Carolyn and Elizabeth expressed doubts about not telling their husbands they were coming. They knew that if they had told of their plans Asa and Andrew would not have agreed. Both women had received letters from them telling of the enormity of overseeing the construction of the division headquarters. It would be like a small city when it was finished to care for the twenty-seven thousand men in the division. Plus, they were enduring and supervising the exhaustive training they were receiving from the French.

As the days to landing shortened, Carolyn and Elizabeth became more questioning as to how they would be received.

One evening they sat in the lounge. Catherine remained in her stateroom.

"It's a good thing we didn't bob our hair," said Elizabeth. "That might be one more deed for them to be upset about. What if they are angry with us, Carolyn?"

"I don't think they are going to be angry. A light reprimand is more like it."

"I've never seen Andrew upset."

"You haven't been married long enough. Asa huffs about at times but it doesn't last."

A boisterous party of three couples came into the room laughing and having a gay old time. They sat in the entertainment area, where they ordered a bottle of champagne from the steward. Elizabeth sat with her back to them while Carolyn had full view.

A paunchy middle-aged man spoke loud enough for Carolyn and Elizabeth to hear. "Edward, you and Victoria should be up on the top deck with us. The government is paying for it."

Edward answered, "Victoria didn't want to be too far from the baby. Seeing we had to drag the maid along we have been relegated to the second-class. Not to my liking."

The color drained from Elizabeth's face.

"What's the matter," whispered Carolyn.

"I know that voice. What does he look like?"

Carolyn discreetly took an inventory of the man they called Edward. She answered in a voice above a whisper, "He is well-dressed, polished shoes, tall, attractive physique, definitely handsome, sandy brown hair…"

"And crystal blue eyes," Elizabeth finished.

Carolyn raised her eyebrows. "How did you know?"

"I've got to get out of here without him seeing me."

"I don't think that's possible."

"Carolyn, that man is Matthew's father!"

Just then one of the gentlemen called, "Would you ladies care to join us?"

Carolyn looked askance and Elizabeth set a determined look. "I might as well face him," she said.

As they started toward the group, the three men rose from their chairs.

Elizabeth placed a counterfeit smile on her face as they neared the group.

Edward almost fell over his chair when he recognized her.

"Thank you for the invitation but we must decline," said Carolyn. "We are about to leave for our staterooms."

The men introduced themselves and their wives. They were going to France on government business.

Carolyn introduced herself. Elizabeth did the same until she came to the man she knew all too well. "Edward and I have met before," she said.

Victoria, Edward's wife, sent a daggered glare in Elizabeth's direction.

With a sweeping glance, Elizabeth could tell this expensively clad woman came from wealth and likely could further Edward's political career.

Elizabeth offered a syrupy smile. "I couldn't help but overhear your conversation. Do I understand you have a child?"

Victoria became the giddy mother. "Oh, yes. Edward and I have a beautiful baby boy. He's only six months old. We couldn't bear to leave him at home."

"How noble. The Edward I knew would not have been considered a model of fatherhood."

A quizzical look crossed Victoria's face. "Whatever do you mean?"

"I'm sure your husband can explain." She turned to the rest of the party. "Enjoy the few sailing days we have left. Shall we go Carolyn?"

There was a hushed silence from those at the table as they watched the two young ladies leave the room.

"Elizabeth, you left them stunned. How do you feel?" whispered Carolyn.

Elizabeth took a deep breath. "I've never felt better. I wonder what the cad is going to offer as an explanation." She rendered a satisfied smile.

They found Catherine awake and reading a book.

"You are not going to believe what just happened," gushed Carolyn.

Catherine closed the book. "Someone made a pass at Elizabeth."

"Worse than that." She related the tale.

"So, if I have put this together right, it seems Mattie's comrade is taking care of Matthew's half-brother. They are the only two black maids on this level."

"That never occurred to me," said a startled Elizabeth.

"What difference does that make?" asked Carolyn. "I was proud of you for keeping a calm demeanor and getting a crack in on Edward. It was long overdue."

Cocking her head and looking up under raised eyelids, a sly smile appeared on Catherine's pleasant face. "Providence at work?"

Chapter 14

Friday, the day of landing, arrived with a flurry of anticipation. Crew members hurried about preparing the ship for docking.

The harbor of Brest, France was filled with boats of every make and size. Passengers crowded to the rails to watch as the big liner made its way through the myriad of sailing vessels.

For the three young women it brought the reality of war to the forefront. The harbor was filled with barges, cruisers, destroyers and United States Navy transports.

There was a heavy mist in the air, but they could make out storage buildings lining the port and the outline of the dingy city behind.

"Look up to the right," said Catherine. "Patrick wrote that he is working out of a building called U. S. Naval Hospital 5. It was a Carmelite convent, and so big it can handle up to five hundred patients."

The women strained to see the stone edifice rising atop a cliff in the foggy mist.

"That looks eerie enough to come from a medieval novel," observed Carolyn.

"I think that is the back of the building. Patrick says there is a railroad in front that carries soldiers to and from the battle zones. He assures me this is a safe area."

"Are they American soldiers?"

"He says most are foreign because we are not into the heat of the combat. Most of our boys in the hospital are training accidents."

Carolyn was still scanning the harbor. "He wouldn't agree to us coming if it wasn't safe."

"Of course it has to be. Otherwise, they wouldn't allow these ocean liners to carry civilians. And what about Edward and those coming on government business? They're not going to put themselves in harm's way," enjoined Elizabeth.

They watched the crowds as the mist cleared but the sky remained overcast.

"I don't see Patrick. We have to wait until he arrives. He could be held up at the hospital."

"There is a throng of people. It may not be easy to spot him," said Carolyn.

It was a few minutes before Mattie exclaimed, "Miz' Catherine, that looks like Mistah' Patrick standin' over there by that buildin'. He's tall and skinny as a beanpole."

Catherine craned her neck in that direction. He looked thinner but snappily dressed in a three piece brown tweed and homburg hat. "It is! Oh, Mattie, I'm so happy." She pulled a handkerchief from her pocketbook and waved it hoping he would wave back. He did.

"He sees us! You get the children ready and stick together so we don't get separated."

When they reached the gangplank, deck hands carried the children. The women followed them down to the solid footing of the dock.

Patrick made his way through the maze of people. He pulled Catherine into his arms and planted a well-received kiss on her welcoming lips.

"Thank God you made it," he whispered in her ear. Then one by one he greeted Carolyn, Elizabeth and Mattie with a hug.

He marveled over the children. "Look how these two have grown," and gave each a gentle pat on the head. "We will have to go inside and wait for your luggage. It may already be there because they were working furiously to get cargo off the ship."

"I believe it will take a few minutes to adjust to walking on land after nine days on that boat," said Catherine. "None of us got seasick and we rather enjoyed the trip."

Patrick kept his arm around her as if never to let her go. "I'm glad," he answered. "Asa and Andrew are under the opinion that the war is going to remain in the eastern part of France and south into Italy, at least for now. That's the reason I agreed to let you come."

They walked to a large warehouse-like building. The cavernous interior was awash with workers, seamen and passengers from other ships. The building served as a starting and ending point for those using the ocean.

As they made their way to the area that held a big HMT CZAR sign, there were two soldiers standing by the booth. They carried their officers' hats tucked under an arm. One was tall and lean with auburn hair, the other stocky built with olive skin and coal black hair.

Elizabeth and Carolyn shouted in unison. "It's Andrew and Asa!"

Forgetting their children, they ran ahead and fell into waiting arms.

Catherine was joyous. "Patrick. You told them."

"Of course I did. But, I didn't tell them until the day you sailed."

"Mattie, it is good you came with us. I believe the mothers forgot all about their children when they saw their men," came Catherine's good-natured admonishment.

"Ain't that the way of it." The big woman gave a gratified smile.

Both couples, in high spirits, hurried back to join the others.

Matthew wiggled out of Mattie's grasp and ran to meet them. Andrew picked him up and swung him around giving him a big kiss. Matthew squiggled around in his father's arms and giggled with joy.

Annie was reticent. She clung to Carolyn's skirt as Asa lowered his husky frame to meet his daughter. "You are my sweet little girl," he said. "Have you forgotten your daddy?" Carolyn leaned down and put an arm around Ann Catherine's waist.

The child looked at her father then quietly put her arms around his neck. Asa picked her up as he stood and held her close. "I was so afraid she

129

would forget me," he said in a voice cracking with hurt. "I can't wait until we get back home."

"Are you upset that we came?" asked Carolyn

"Upset? How could that be possible? This is the grandest Christmas present I could ever hope for."

Carolyn looped her arm through Asa's and turned to Elizabeth. "See? I told you they wouldn't be angry."

"I'm still waiting for the reprimand," joshed Elizabeth.

"Never," answered Andrew and pulled her close.

"How free are you men?" asked Patrick. "I am pulling an evening shift at the hospital so I need to be back by three. I thought we could get the ladies settled and have a bite to eat before I have to resume my duties."

"We have coverage until five o'clock but it will take us close to an hour to get back to base."

Andrew looked at Patrick. "I'm ready to see the place you secured. How did that happen to come your way?"

"A mother brought her son to the hospital for a minor ailment. She's English and said she was going to England for the holidays. It seems her husband is a French general stationed in Paris. I told her my wife and her friends were coming from America and she offered her house in Liffol le Grand. I haven't seen it, but I didn't want them staying in Brest. Poor sanitary conditions."

Andrew concurred. "I agree with you there. We've run into some of the same problems in Neufchateau setting up the headquarters. I guess we'll have to wait and see if this place will hold everyone and what kind of condition it's in."

Patrick defended his choice. "I figured a general's house wouldn't be a shack."

"After the cramped cabins on the ship, I believe we can squeeze into anything," came Carolyn's opinion.

Asa had left the group taking Ann Catherine with him. He motioned for them to come to where he stood.

"The luggage is here. We can load it into the truck and be on our way."

"Truck!" was Elizabeth's immediate reaction.

"We didn't think a car would fit all of us plus the paraphernalia ladies like to carry," said a good-natured Andrew. "This will be a new experience. I told you life with me would be exciting."

"Riding in a truck doesn't sound like the excitement I envisioned," Elizabeth replied and kissed his cheek.

The group waited in front of the warehouse in the cool air waiting for Asa to drive up. He arrived in a big military truck with an arched canvas covered bed.

"We can haul almost thirty soldiers in that," informed Andrew. "Ready for an adventure?"

The women stood in disbelief.

"We'll load your belongings in first and then help you ladies up," ordered Andrew. "Patrick will have to ride in the cab with Asa because he has the directions. I'll ride in the back."

"Wouldn't it be easier to get up there with a step-stool?" asked a practical Catherine.

"We didn't think to bring one. The men just jump in. I'll get up and give you a hand up." He leaped his lithe and agile frame into the truck bed. "See, that's how it's done."

"I think you're showing off, Andrew," Elizabeth said, trying to hide the pride she held for her noble soldier.

"Hand the children up, then give me your hand."

Asa and Patrick came onto the scene after discussing the road to travel.

With a hand up and a helpful boost, the women were settled. Mattie took some extra encouragement and extra strength, but she took her place beside Catherine.

"We will only be about a mile from Brest so you won't have to endure this ride too long," offered a reassuring Patrick.

"After that bone-jolting farm wagon, I can tolerate anything," said Carolyn.

The road to Liffol le Grand was hard-packed dirt until they reached the small town where the street became cobblestone.

If it had been a warm, sunshiny day, it might have been a pretty scene. The rumbling of the truck, the cool, damp weather and the bleakness of a winter landscape was not a welcoming feeling. The women were silent.

Andrew sat next to Elizabeth holding her hand with Matthew perched on his lap.

Through the middle of the town, they spied small shops housed in stone buildings lining the street, and a massive Catholic church with a spire that seemed to reach to the sky.

"This used to be an old Roman town," informed Andrew over the roar of the engine. "Only about fifteen hundred people lived here before we camped the 1st and 3rd Battalions outside of town. The Machine Gun Battalion is a about a mile away."

"Don't the people resent you being here?" asked Catherine.

"Our being here has helped their business and they want the war to stay away. They consider us rescuers."

The truck started to climb away from the flat land and up a steep incline. They sat with both hands clenching onto the bench seats along the sides of the truck as the vehicle climbed. At times, it seemed as if the incline was too much for the lumbering machine, and they could feel the grinding of gears as Asa adeptly powered it along until it came to a jerking halt.

Patrick and Asa came to the rear of the truck.

"Here we are, ladies."

After alighting from the bed of the truck, they were awed by the sight of a stone French villa with arched windows and leaded glass panes. The second story held French doors that opened onto individual balconies. Flowerless window boxes adorned the windows.

"It must be magnificent in the summer," remarked Elizabeth.

"Do you have the key, Patrick?" asked Catherine.

"The lady said someone would be here to let us in."

They walked to the massive wooden front doors and pulled a cord that sounded a loud bell.

The door was opened by a middle-aged French woman.

Patrick tipped his homburg. "We are here at Mrs. Du Charme's invitation."

The woman looked at a loss and spoke in French.

Elizabeth stepped forward and answered in the same dialect.

"You speak French?" asked a surprised Andrew. "Why didn't you tell me?"

"I don't recall you ever asking." She addressed the rest of the party. "This is Celeste. She said the lady of the house told her that she is to stay here and take care of the house."

"Do you mean cook meals and clean?" asked Carolyn.

Elizabeth posed the question to the woman.

"She said she is to take care of all our needs. She has a man to help, and we should come in out of the damp cold."

"I'm for that," said Asa. "Let's get these little ones inside before they catch cold."

"I've never had a maid to wait on me," remarked Carolyn. "I won't know how to act."

"Don't get spoiled," said Asa with a half-grin.

Inside the house was a large, sunken room two stories high. The room was richly adorned in French style furniture. At the end was a large fireplace with a roaring fire that warmed the interior. Around the room was a railing and hallway on both floors with doors opening into rooms on both sides.

The group stood in amazement. "I never expected this," said Patrick. "Mrs. Du Charme wouldn't hear of me paying for it because she didn't want it empty and looking like a target for looters. Word in a small town gets around."

"You don't have to tell us that," said Catherine. "Elizabeth, will you ask the maid about bedrooms?"

"She says there are four bedrooms. Two on the right and two on the left of this split staircase."

"You and Elizabeth should be on the same side," Catherine said to Carolyn. "Mattie and I will take the other side. Let's get this luggage up to its rightful place so we can relax."

The bedrooms were as well appointed as the downstairs. Each had a private sitting area and French doors that opened onto a balcony that overlooked the town of Liffol le Grand.

135

As was their nature, Carolyn and Elizabeth had to inspect all rooms before they were satisfied with which side of the house to settle in. Catherine stood back and let them stake their claim before she and Mattie went to the opposite side.

The men dutifully carried their belongings.

Once inside their private room, Catherine turned to Patrick. "I believe Providence was looking out for us. I have so much to tell you that I couldn't write in letters."

"I believe that will have to wait because that bed looks inviting." He drew her into his arms and started unbuttoning her lace-front blouse.

"Patrick, it's the middle of the day."

"So it is," he agreed as he drew her nearer and plied her with warm kisses. "I haven't had the pleasure of your company for three months, and I am going to make the most of it."

"It has been a long three months," she said and succumbed to his charms.

An hour later, Patrick was checking his pocket watch.

Catherine lazed in the bed as she admired this caring man she had married. "How are you going to get back to Brest?"

"Asa said he will drive me down. They'll have to be leaving soon. It's almost one o'clock."

"Maybe there is something downstairs that we can conjure up for lunch. You shouldn't go back to the hospital without eating. I noticed you've lost weight."

"The place keeps me on the run. The others may be downstairs by now." He sent a sly smile to his agreeable wife. "Don't think Asa and Andrew didn't have the same idea I had. I noticed they sent the children with Mattie."

A half-hour later they found the kitchen. Celeste scooted them out of the room and led them to the dining room where four smiling faces greeted them.

"Patrick, old boy, you couldn't have found a more accommodating place," complimented Andrew. "Nothing like a renewal of the spirit!"

Elizabeth turned a delicate pink.

Carolyn smiled and took Asa's hand. "I agree. Catherine, look what Celeste has prepared: chicken, rice, carrots and apple cream pie."

"If we take time to eat, it'll be almost two before we leave," said Patrick. "Will that be enough time to get me back to Brest and you to Neufchateau?"

"As long as the truck behaves and we don't get stuck in a rut," answered Asa. "That's a mighty narrow lane leading up to this place."

"You did a masterful job of getting that truck up here. For a time, I thought we were going to roll back down that steep grade." Carolyn's eyes were full of admiration.

"When we landed, it rained for days. Horses and mules were up to their knees in mud. We had to learn how to traverse these primitive roads."

"Similar to some of those farm roads in Clarke County," came Elizabeth's tongue-in-cheek reply.

The mention of home made them smile.

Chapter 15

The next morning greeted those at the villa with sunshine. On that winter day, Celeste prepared their breakfast of French bread, creamed eggs and cheese souffle'.

The women took their places at the dining room table. Mattie was reluctant to sit with them. "Miz' Catherine, this don' seem right. I should be out there helpin' in the kitchen."

"Mattie, we are not in Georgetown, and we are all guests. Celeste is as protective of her kitchen as you are of ours at home. This should be a welcome change for you."

"It jus' don't seem right."

"You came to take care of the children. That is enough to keep you busy," Catherine said with finality.

Carolyn was amiable. "Mattie, enjoy the attention. I plan to because I don't have anyone to wait on me at home. When we get back, it will be the same old grind."

Mattie wagged her head and took a seat.

"It's three days before Christmas. I wonder how the French celebrate?" questioned Elizabeth.

"You should know. You said you took three years of French in that fancy school you went to," answered Carolyn.

Elizabeth sent a disgusted look in Carolyn's direction. "We studied the language not the customs."

"It's Saturday and I'm sure the shops will be closed tomorrow. Why don't we walk down into town and see what it has to offer," suggested Catherine. "Perhaps we can find a present for the children and some treats for all of us."

Once breakfast was over, they dressed in their warm coats, hats and gloves and started down the long drive that led from the villa to the town. They were up so high they could make out the chimneys of Brest less than a mile away.

Catherine shadowed her eyes from the bright sun. "I told Patrick I wanted to visit the hospital, but he wouldn't allow it. He said the sanitary conditions are deplorable and they are getting many cases of Spanish flu."

"Oh, darn! I had hoped to tour the hospital," said a disappointed Carolyn. "They have Red Cross Nurses working there. I still haven't given up on coming over and lending my services."

"I think you had better discuss that with Asa. He's not going to agree. You're just talking through your hat."

Elizabeth kicked a piece of dead leaves coated with ice out of the way with her boot. "I certainly changed my mind the minute we landed. Washington may be a dirty city in spots, but it certainly beats the city of Brest. I didn't care for those dock workers ogling us as we went by."

"I believe they were captivated by you, Elizabeth. Your blonde hair and blue eyes stand out. I've noticed most of the women here have my coloring," said Carolyn.

"It wasn't just me. Their eyes followed you and Catherine also. It gave me a creepy feeling."

They rounded a curve and waited as Mattie's huge presence, followed by the two toddlers, came into view.

Carolyn laughed. "Maybe it was Mattie who caught their attention. I'm sure we were a conversation piece traipsing down the street."

"Not only did they openly stare when we passed by, but they watched us climb into that awful military truck. It was embarrassing."

"Elizabeth, be grateful we didn't have to walk to the villa," Catherine said.

"That brings to mind," enjoined Carolyn. "We are going to have to climb up this hill on our way back. It must be half-a-mile."

Mattie and the children caught up to the waiting group.

"I hadn't thought of that,' admitted Elizabeth.

"We'll just have to take our time," said Catherine.

The town of Liffol le Grand was at the foot of the long hill. Little children played in the streets in badly worn clothing and there were a few French women coming and going in and out of the stores. In front of some of the shops, bottles of wine and beer, aged cheeses and dried herbs were displayed in the cool morning air.

Catherine assumed the role of leader. "Here we are. Let's venture forth and see how we're received. Elizabeth stay close. We'll need you to interpret for us."

Elizabeth spied an area that held park benches and teeter-totters. "Mattie, there's a small park over there. You can take the children there to play while we see what the shops have to offer."

"Miz' Elizabeth. If it's all the same to you, I'll tag along and watch these two."

"Wouldn't it be easier to let them run in the park?"

"Elizabeth, have you seen another colored person since we landed?" asked Catherine.

"No."

"Then I think Mattie will be more comfortable staying with us."

Elizabeth blushed. "I am sorry. How insensitive of me."

The cobblestone street was narrow with pebbled sidewalks on both sides.

They passed a cobbler's shop, barber shop, meat market, pharmacy and bake shop before entering a larger store that held a variety of goods.

"We should buy a present for Celeste," said Elizabeth.

"Of course," the others agreed.

They fingered silk scarves, lace collars and leather gloves before settling on a bottle of expensive perfume.

Elizabeth handled the transaction using American money. "The clerk says that with all the American troops in France the bank is happy to accept American dollars."

When they left the shop, Carolyn whispered to Elizabeth, "I saw Mattie eyeing that purple atomizer filled with Chanel perfume. Why don't you go back in there and buy it? That will be our gift for taking care of the children."

The plan appealed to Elizabeth. "Catherine where do you want to go next?"

"I'd like to stop in that wine shop."

"Agreed," said Elizabeth. "You go ahead and I'll catch up with you."

"What if we need you to talk to the store-keeper?"

"Just stall for time. I'll only be a couple of minutes."

Catherine shrugged her shoulders. "It must be important."

"It is," said Carolyn. "Let's be on our way."

When they reached the little stone shop, Mattie halted the children. "Miz' Catherine. How about the little ones stay out here with me while you all go inside? There's plenty of room on this bench, an' that little place jus' looks like it ain't a place for busy hands."

"That's a wise choice," said Carolyn.

The two women went inside. The wine shop was dimly lit and cool. The short, swarthy, middle-aged man behind the counter greeted them in broken English. "Good afternoon."

"You speak English," remarked a relieved Catherine.

"A little. I have learned some from the soldiers. First the English and now the Americans. Our young men are all gone fighting in this terrible war."

"We would like to buy some wine for Christmas."

"A lady's wine or a gentleman's?"

"Both," answered Carolyn.

She looked around and was drawn to a large wheel of aged cheese. "We would also like two pounds of that cheese and a bag of soda crackers."

Elizabeth entered the shop carrying two large parcels.

"It looks like you bought out the store. We're in luck because this man speaks English, at least well enough that we can understand," remarked Carolyn.

"I found a couple other things. You may have to help me carry one of these packages back up to the villa."

"I'm dying to see what you bought. We have wine, cheese and crackers to celebrate Christmas," said a pleased Carolyn.

"Wonderful. Let's buy some of those nuts and some chocolates."

"I'm not sure we can afford what we've already picked out," said a concerned Catherine.

"Of course we can. Andrew left extra money. He said that it is Christmas and we should enjoy ourselves." Elizabeth held up a box of chocolates and spoke to the owner in French. He shook his head. She said something else in a questioning tone. He shook his head again. Once more Elizabeth posed a question followed by her most alluring smile. The man brightened and nodded his agreement.

They gathered their bounty and went out the door.

Catherine used a stern voice, "Elizabeth were you bargaining with him?"

"I most certainly was. I discovered in the last shop that the local ladies were arguing over prices. The shop clerk told me bargaining was expected. She also confided that the soldiers haven't caught on yet so when they come into town it's a happy time."

"Well done," complimented Carolyn. "Let's hit the pastry shop next."

Once they were through shopping they sat on benches lining the sidewalk.

"Have you noticed there are no decorations for Christmas except for some red ribbons tied around? I haven't seen even a suggestion of a Christmas tree," mused Elizabeth.

"There has been a war going on. I don't know how they celebrate, but my guess is they will buy only necessities," summed up Catherine's thought on the subject.

"I dread walking up that big hill," said Elizabeth. "Perhaps I should not have been so zealous in buying."

"Too late now. I can't wait to see what is in those packages," declared an exuberant Carolyn. "We'll take turns carrying them."

"Maybe we can rent a cart," was the practical Catherine's suggestion.

While they sat contemplating their dilemma, a U.S. Army vehicle came down the street. The square-shaped, drab-colored small vehicle came to an abrupt stop in front of the women. A hefty young soldier jumped out.

"I ain't seen such a group of good-lookin' American women in months," he said, flashing a wide grin.

"How did you know we were American?" asked Catherine. "We could be English."

"Nope. Gotta' be American 'cause you got your colored nanny with ya'."

Mattie glowered at the brash young man.

Carolyn spoke up, "You may do us a service. We need a ride up that long lane leading to the big house up on the hill."

The soldier craned his neck to spot the villa and gave a low whistle. "Whoa. That's a hard climb for this cranky car."

"Obviously, it isn't big enough for all of us," Catherine chimed in. "If you could take these packages, the children and their nanny, we would be most appreciative."

Mattie sent a wry look and sideways glance at Catherine.

The soldier scratched his head. "Well, I ain't sure."

Carolyn spoke up. "Where are you stationed, soldier?"

"Over at Neufchateau. I was on my way back."

"Then I am sure you are acquainted with Major Thomas and Major Caldwell."

The young man raised his eyebrows. "Major Thomas is my commanding officer."

She assumed a lofty air. "I am the major's wife. I don't believe he would be pleased to hear that one of his soldiers did not lend me a hand when I needed it."

The young man perked up. "No ma'am, but it'll take two trips and it might make me late in gettin' back to base. The major ain't gonna' like that."

"I'll vouch for you. The major will be grateful. Now, help us load up so you can be on your way."

Off he went with his carload of packages, two little children and a disgusted Mattie looking back at the three women.

Elizabeth was aglow with admiration, "Carolyn, you do know how to get your way."

Catherine was delighted with the prospect of not trudging up that long hill. "I believe we have enough time for a cup of tea."

With a lightened step, they went into the warm little café to wait for the reluctant soldier's return.

Chapter 16

Sunday was another cloudy day. It was also the day when Patrick, Asa and Andrew would arrive so the women were jubilant despite the overcast day.

The military officers came astride horses that were as impressive as the men that rode them. Claude, the man who helped Celeste care for the place, met them when they rode in. He took the reins and led the horses to the barn. He was a quiet young man with average looks, who most likely would have been in the French army except for a limp and one slouched shoulder. He kept himself busy around the barn and helping Celeste when she called for him, which she did with a loud clanging on a big enamel dishpan. The visiting women had gotten used to the sound, although it unnerved them when they first heard it.

Carolyn was playing with Annie in her bedroom when she spied horses coming up the lane. She hollered to Elizabeth, who was in the next room.

Elizabeth grabbed Matthew's hand and headed for the stairs.

The four of them scurried down the flight and met Asa and Andrew at the door.

It was another grand welcoming of hugs and kisses before they made their way to the large living area where Claude had a roaring fire going in the massive stone fireplace.

"Why did you come on horseback?" asked Elizabeth.

"The horses needed exercise and so did we," answered Andrew with a wide grin.

"We couldn't buy, beg or steal a car," replied a truthful Asa. "We have the promise of one tomorrow because there will be no training exercises until the day after Christmas. We'll ride back tomorrow morning, return with a car and take you ladies to the base."

"For the day?" asked Carolyn.

Annie was perched on Asa's knee playing with the medals on his uniform. "For the day. But, I suggest you leave the little ones here with Mattie. We want to show you the headquarters and the training grounds. It would be a tiring day for them."

"Mattie has been a God-send," informed Elizabeth. "She came along to take care of the children so we could spend time with you. I'm not sure it is an enjoyable trip for her."

Catherine appeared on the stairs. "I thought I heard glad voices. When did you arrive?" She greeted the men, who stood when she entered. "Patrick expects to be here around four."

"It's close to that now," said Andrew. "Too bad we couldn't get a car, we could take you ladies to the theatre in Neufchateau. They are having a concert of Christmas music."

150

"Oh, that would be glorious," exclaimed Elizabeth.

Carolyn was not so thrilled. "I, for one, would not look forward to driving up that narrow lane on a dark night. We could plunge down the hill."

Catherine could not contain her chance to tease. "Why, Carolyn. Have you lost your sense of adventure?"

Before she could answer, they were interrupted by the sound of the bell at the front door. Patrick had arrived.

Catherine hurried to the door where she gladly received him with open arms.

"That's a mighty tug up that hill." He removed his outer coat and hat.

"You walked from Brest?"

He laughed. "It's not quite two miles. I think it was faster than taking that military truck. I must be out of shape because I was winded when I came up the lane."

"Patrick, you are working too hard. You've not only lost weight you can't afford to lose, but you also look tired."

He put his arm around her waist and pulled her close. "I have this evening and two days after to rest up. I told them I would be back the day after Christmas."

They walked to where the others were gathered in conversation.

Asa and Andrew rose to meet them. They shook hands with Patrick before he and Catherine took a seat together on a silk brocade settee.

"We're making plans for tomorrow," said Andrew. "We are thinking about making a day of it over at the base. Would you and Catherine like to join us?"

Patrick did not hesitate. "I'm for it. What do you say, Catherine? Are you up to a day in Neufchateau? I hear it is a charming town."

So much for Patrick getting rest, thought Catherine before nodding her agreement.

"Settled then," said Andrew. "Asa and I will bring a car after we take our horses back. We can spend the day and return back here to the villa before it gets dark. I wouldn't want to plunge down the side of the hill."

"Jest if you want, Andrew. But, you cannot deny that it is a possibility. Besides, it feels like it's going to snow," said a chagrined Carolyn.

Asa laughed. "How do you know it's going to snow?"

"Trust me. I'm an old country girl."

"Shouldn't we have a little Christmas tree or something to remind us that it is Christmas?" asked Elizabeth. "I miss seeing lights and trees and decorated shops. Maybe we should go to Paris. They have the best clothing designers."

They all looked at her in wonderment.

Andrew's gentle voice broke the spell. "My dear, Paris is over a hundred miles east of here not to mention there is a war going on."

With a smile of embarrassment, she said, "I guess that takes care of that idea."

Asa stood up. "We most certainly should have a tree. Let's hunt up Claude and see if he has an axe we can borrow."

The men returned before supper with a three-foot fir tree. The young man had not only lent them an axe, but he had nailed a crisscross of boards together with a hole in the center to stabilize the tree.

With a sense of excitement, the onlookers watched with anticipation as Asa set their prize on a table in the gathering room. Unfortunately, their enthusiasm dwindled when they realized the small bare tree looked more like a twig in the cavernous room.

Matthew was engrossed with the presence of the tree and did his best to reach up and grab at the limbs.

Annie wasn't quite sure what to make of it. She put her arms up for Asa to hold her.

They walked around the room and cocked their heads. Maybe the lonesome little tree would look better from a different angle.

"We will have to do something to dress it up as soon as supper is over," remarked Carolyn.

Celeste rang the bell for mealtime. All nine of them sat around the long dining table in the inviting room painted white with gold trim. Blue brocade drapes hung at the windows and a crystal chandelier hung from the etched tin ceiling.

"The French general must make a good salary," remarked Asa.

"Mrs. Du Charme was quite the lady so I suspect there is English money also," Patrick replied.

"And, we must all be thankful," said Catherine. "After seeing the surrounding area, we could be holed up in two rooms or suffer the dingy city of Brest."

"I propose a toast to General and Mrs. Du Charme," announced Andrew as he raised his glass of wine.

"To General and Mrs. Du Charme!" came their chorus of voices.

Mattie continued helping the children with their food.

After supper it was time to decorate the tree. They made strings of threaded popcorn and draped them on the branches. Elizabeth used a delicate white lace shawl for a tree skirt. Carolyn attached a few of Annie's hair ribbons and Catherine made a tinfoil star to put on the top.

When they were done, they clapped at the results of their ingenuity.

"This will be a Christmas we will always remember," said Catherine with a bit of nostalgia.

Mattie took the little ones to the nursery where she also slept. It was a big room overlooking the view toward the town of Liffol le Grand. The children were happy there playing with toys owned by the Du Charme children, and Mattie was happy to have a place of seclusion when she wished to be away from the rest of the party.

Catherine knew she must tell Patrick about the miscarriage. How would he react to the news? Regardless, she had to tell him before Carolyn and Elizabeth told their husbands and the word accidently slipped out.

They had retired for the night and were lounging in bed. "Patrick, I have sad news for you."

He turned on his side, propped on his elbow, and his questioning eyes searched her face. "Sad news?"

"Early in November, Carolyn, Elizabeth and I took a trip to Berryville."

He smiled. "There must be more. So far it doesn't sound sad."

"The reason we went was so that I could see Dr. Hawthorne."

He sat up. "Were you ill?"

She pulled herself up to sit beside him. She swallowed hard. "I was expecting a baby."

He gave a start and gazed at her deeply before he put his arm around her. She rested her head on his shoulder.

"Tell me what happened," he encouraged.

Catherine unfolded the story.

"You must have known before I left. Why didn't you tell me? I would have stayed."

Catherine felt close to tears. "It wouldn't have been fair to you. Dr. Hawthorne is the best

155

baby doctor around. He said there was nothing anyone could do."

"But, I could have been there for you. You should have told me."

"Are you angry with me?"

He pulled her closer. "Of course I'm not angry with you. It must have been a very difficult time."

He understood! Catherine was relieved and gained her self-control. "It was a blessing to have Carolyn and Elizabeth, and the Hawthornes were wonderful. I want this war to be over so we can settle down and raise a family."

His kiss was gentle. "I am so sorry."

They lay back on the bed nestled in each other's arms.

"I have been thinking," he said. "I believe I will be coming home after my six months is up."

She turned to look at him. "Six months? You didn't tell me about six months."

"No, because I was prepared to stay until the end of the war. Volunteers signed up for six months duty. I figured I would extend the time if I needed to."

"Oh, Patrick. That would mean you would be coming home in April!"

"I came to gain experience. Although, the injured Americans I am treating are mostly accidents or usual illnesses, I am getting plenty of experience with the allied soldiers. A man is a man no matter what uniform he wears."

"You are so wise. I can bear the loneliness as long as I have an end in sight." She rolled over and wrapped her arms around him. "I've made a confession and so have you. I am deliriously happy. Let's not waste what's left of this lovely night."

He laughed and cupped her face in his hands. "Mrs. Burke, you are a wonder."

Chapter 17

Neufchateau was a larger village than Liffol Le Grand. The three couples arrived in a covered carriage, a prized possession of the villa, driven by Claude. When Elizabeth had informed him of their plans, it was he who suggested using the carriage. He was more than pleased to get away from the continual orders from Celeste. As long as it was for the visitors, he was allowed to go.

Asa and Andrew directed him south of the town where military training took place, except for today as all training had been canceled until the day after Christmas.

On arrival at the training grounds, the women drew in their breath when they left the carriage. The terrain was ugly, flat and treeless with hills in the distance. The land was pock-marked by grenade practice and trenches dug into the ground.

Accustomed to being in charge, Asa acted as guide. "This is called the Noncourt Sector. Named after the village of Noncourt. The French have named the trenches after our New England boys: Trenche de Boston, Trenche de Newport, Trenche de New Haven. Each trench has a specific job: front line of observation, line of resistance and line of support." He waved his arm in another direction. "That's where the British train our troops in bayonet fighting and hand-to-hand combat."

"Are we allowed to go into one of the trenches?" asked Carolyn.

"If you want."

"Count me out," said Elizabeth. "The landscape is enough. I'm going back and sit in the carriage until it's time to go back to town."

Andrew walked with her. "I didn't realize this would upset you."

"It is too vivid for my imagination. I worry about you and the condition of these training grounds insures my doubts that you will remain safe."

"Perhaps it was a mistake to bring you out here. You'll feel better once you see what we've accomplished setting up the headquarters."

They climbed into the carriage. Her blue eyes searched his face. "Tell me honestly, Andrew. Will you only be here for six months? That is the hope that Carolyn and I cling to."

"I was sure when we began, but now I am uncertain. Our allies are war-weary and their ranks dwindle each day. We are here as ancillary troops. That may change."

She contemplated his words in silence.

"Andrew, I have been to visit your parents at Red Gate Farm."

He gave a look of surprise. "Did you go by yourself?"

"Catherine, Carolyn and I went to Berryville. We stayed in my apartment over the hat shop, which, by the way, still hasn't had a buyer." She was uncertain if she should tell their reason for

159

going but she did. "Don't breathe a word of this or act differently once you know. Catherine was expecting a baby and she had a miscarriage while we were there."

"How sad for them," he said. "She seems healthy."

"She is back to the Catherine we love. It was a traumatic experience for all of us."

"I can imagine." He took her hand in his.

"That isn't all the bad news. Your mother has had a set-back. Dr. Hawthorne thinks it may have been an apoplectic shock."

"Oh no! How is she?"

"She has weakness on one side and they are using a wheelchair, but she seemed to understand much of what was going on. She wasn't able to speak. I'll go to see her after we get back home. They will be glad to have news of you."

"Damn this war! I hope they understand there wasn't time to get out there once I received orders." He rested his head on the back of the seat.

"Emily asked if Matthew and I would come and live there until you returned."

He lifted his head. "Good for Emily. She could use some company. Would you consider making that change?"

"I put it right out of my mind. But, I've had second thoughts. I am not pleased living with my parents. Matthew and I can occupy your upstairs living quarters. It would almost be like having a part of you there with us."

"Wouldn't you miss being near the city? And, you would be away from Catherine and Carolyn. It could be a lonely time for you."

"I've given that thought. Mother still tries to run my life and I believe it confuses Matthew. I'm not sure he knows whether it is Mother or I who's in charge."

He gave a troubled sigh. "I'm sorry a house wasn't available on base. I felt guilty having to leave you at your parents' home."

"Catherine is always talking about Providence intervening. This may be one of those times. I have a gnawing feeling that I need to be at Red Gate Farm until you come home."

He reached for her hand. "You make the decision that will work the best for you. I know my parents would welcome having you there. I do love you, Elizabeth." His kiss was warm and gentle.

The carriage door opened. "So this is why you decided to exit the tour," said Carolyn as she caught them in a tight embrace.

"It beats exploring trenches," quipped Andrew.

The two couples climbed in before Claude turned the horses around and headed north toward town.

"You were wise, Elizabeth," said Catherine. "There was nothing glamorous about scaling down a ladder into a dirty mud-hole. I can feel the grit between my teeth."

"We're going to stop by headquarters before we get into town," advised Asa. "This will brighten your spirits."

A few minutes later, Claude stopped the carriage. An entirely different sight greeted the passengers. As far as they could see there were buildings, telephone lines, barracks and row upon row of tents.

Claude had parked the carriage at the railroad station that was used to transport troops and supplies. The women saw warehouse after warehouse and were awed at the enormity of the undertaking to erect these headquarters.

They left the carriage and walked the hard-packed, dirt main street where they passed: repair shops, machine shop, military police station, field hospital, bathing and clothing unit, commissary, bakery company, and laundry company.

"Were you in charge of all this?" asked Carolyn in disbelief.

Asa smiled. "We were in charge of seeing that everyone performed their jobs. We are waiting to get a veterinary hospital, which I hope is coming soon. We depend on our horses and mules and we need to keep them in top shape."

"I'd like to see your field hospital," said Patrick. "I am not pleased with the sanitary conditions in Brest."

"That has been one of our biggest problems in the whole headquarters. The engineers have done their best to handle the sewage, but we still get cases of dysentery. It's safer to drink the wine than the water."

While they stood surveying the area, a soldier passed by, saluted the officers and walked on. There was a brindle bull terrier at his heels dressed in its own Army uniform.

"My goodness," said Catherine, "that little dog is as military and upright as the soldiers."

Andrew laughed. "That's Stubby, mascot of the 102nd Regiment. He was smuggled aboard the USS Mississippi and when he reached here the Commander gave him a reprieve. He's a remarkable dog because in the training field he has learned the bugle calls and marching drills."

The women looked at each other. What other surprises were in store?

"Asa, why don't you escort Patrick over to the hospital while I take the ladies into the YMCA for a cup of tea?" suggested Andrew.

They stood in front of a building and watched three women dressed in snappy blue hats and uniforms go in the front door.

"Who are they?" asked Elizabeth.

Andrew answered. "They are from the Army Signal Corps. We call them the "Hello Girls" because they man the telephone communications. They must speak fluent French and English."

"Of course." said Elizabeth. "I thought of applying for that position at one time. They train at the Signal School at Camp Franklin, Maryland. They receive military training as well as learning to be radio and switchboard operators. Unfortunately, one has to be over 25."

Andrew's look was not kind. "You have no business even thinking of such a thing."

Carolyn sensed Elizabeth's discomfort and was quick to step in. "I thought of joining the Army Nurse Corps."

Asa's head snapped around from talking with Patrick. "That I wouldn't allow. We have Ann Catherine and she needs a mother."

Catherine was uncomfortable with the whole tone of conversation. "Well, I guess we've settled those foolhardy ideas. I say we have that tea Andrew offered."

"You go ahead," Asa agreed. "Patrick and I will visit the hospital and meet all of you at the Y."

"Asa would you mind if I accompanied you to the hospital?" asked a polite Carolyn.

"Of course I wouldn't mind. I believe you will find it different than the nursing you are used to."

Off they went.

Andrew found a comfortable table in the YMCA building away from the admiring eyes of the soldiers, who were playing ping pong and shooting pool. They all did a double-take when the women walked by. He seated the ladies and went in quest of a pot of hot tea.

Forty-five minutes later, Asa, Patrick and Carolyn arrived and took seats at the table.

Carolyn was in a subdued mood.

"What was your impression of the hospital?" asked Catherine.

"It was depressing," answered Carolyn. "They are short on staff and supplies, but not short of young, injured soldiers. Some who may never see their home again."

"Have some tea," offered a sympathetic Catherine. "The pot is still plenty warm." She poured a cup for her friend. "Would you gentlemen care for a cup?"

They declined.

Asa checked his pocket watch. "We should be on our way into town if you want to get some shopping in before we have to head back."

"I'll scout up the driver," said Andrew.

"Let's all go," said Carolyn. "A walk will do us good." Carolyn hoped a walk in the open air would clear her head of the visions remaining from her visit to the hospital.

Claude was waiting at the train station where they had left him. Either he didn't feel welcome in the soldiers' area or he was afraid someone might run off with the carriage. It was of no concern to the passengers. They were happy to rest their tired feet.

After leaving the headquarters they found Neufchateau a welcoming town. The town square held a huge fountain with a trickle of running water. Asa explained that was to keep the fountain from freezing up in the winter.

Little shops surrounded the square. The focal point was a lovely, ornate theatre with a wide

165

set of stone steps across the front. They served as an entrance and also for town gatherings of importance or performance. Two churches overpowered the two-story buildings below.

Here the women were delighted to see men, women and children bustling about. If there were cares about a war, they were not evident. The town apparently thrived from the influx of soldiers with American money.

Shops were decorated with greenery, red ribbons and colorful glass baubles igniting the feeling of Christmas for the three young women far from home.

They decided they should buy a gift for Claude

"Let's buy him some warm gloves," suggested Elizabeth. "Have you noticed how worn his look?"

"How about a bottle of brandy? He can hide it in the barn and take a swig when he gets the urge," enjoined Andrew.

"It would take a man to think of that," said Carolyn. "You men buy the brandy and we will purchase some nice gloves."

"Agreed," said Patrick. "I've been observing his limp. I'm not sure if he has a spinal problem or if one leg is shorter than the other. If that's the case, it can be solved by adding a platform to his shoe."

"How would you approach that without offending him?" asked Asa.

"Elizabeth could help," came Catherine's enthusiastic reply. "From the way he looks at her, I believe he would do anything for her."

"That's only because I speak his language," was Elizabeth's quick response.

"No it isn't. I've noticed it too," said Carolyn.

"Who can resist my darling wife? Let's tackle the Claude problem later," said Andrew. "We'll need to be on our way within the hour or we might be in danger of plunging off Carolyn's cliff."

They hurried about and wished they had more time, but the church belfry announced five o'clock with the playing of chimes.

The group gathered up their packages and found the carriage parked in front of a tavern. Five of them climbed into the carriage while Andrew made his way to the bar where Claude was finishing a whiskey. It was obvious it wasn't the only one he had downed. Andrew signaled they were ready for the ride back to the villa. Claude waved to the barmaid and weaved out the door.

Andrew poked his head into the carriage. "Asa, you may have to drive. Claude is a bit tipsy."

"Look," observed Carolyn. "It's starting to snow. I knew it."

Asa got out of the carriage and helped Andrew push Claude inside. The young Frenchman offered a guilty smile to Elizabeth, fell into the seat next to her, and promptly fell asleep with his head on her shoulder.

Andrew laughed. "I'll ride up with you, Asa. My seat's been taken."

It was beginning to get dark when they reached the villa an hour and a half later. Snow was falling in earnest. Asa parked the carriage at the front door. Claude awoke groggy, but he climbed out of the back and the cold air seemed to revive him. He said something to Elizabeth before he took the driver's seat and headed to the barn.

"What did he say?" asked Andrew.

"He said he has never had such a wonderful day."

They all chuckled.

It was Christmas Eve and the house was alive with delightful aromas emanating from the kitchen. Celeste told Elizabeth that the French celebrate with midnight Mass and enjoy a big dinner afterward. She decided to cook the big dinner for them when they arrived home because she knew they would be hungry.

A feast it was and they were famished: roast goose, plates of cheeses and breads, greens and potatoes in a gravy sauce, fried stuffed mushrooms, dried fruits and assorted French pastries. Of course this food was accompanied by a variety of wines. They ate and drank and laughed and toasted until they were drained of energy and retired for the night.

Claude was right. It had been a wonderful day.

Chapter 18

Christmas Day was met with gladness and sadness. It was their last day together. Patrick would resume his duties at the hospital, Asa and Andrew would commence their grueling days in the Army, and the young women would pack up their belongings for the long trip home.

Catherine arose early. She slipped out of bed, donned a warm robe to ward off the chill of the room and looked out the second story window. The snow had melted and left puddles of water. The day was misty. They had one day of sunshine since they had landed and she wondered if France always looked so overcast and disheartening.

Catherine was engrossed in writing in her diary when she heard, "That must be important to drive you from a warm bed."

She turned and smiled at the man who had stolen her heart. Patrick looked less tired and troubled than when he had met her on the wharf. His dark brown hair was cut neatly and his lean face clean shaven. She had missed his kind and thoughtful ways.

"If I don't write down the events of each day, I will forget. This will be a comfort to me when I get home. It will be like reliving these few priceless days we have enjoyed."

"They have been rejuvenating," Patrick agreed.

Catherine removed her robe and crawled into bed beside him. "There is one thing troubling me. Dare I ask?"

He pulled her close. "Ask away."

"This Mrs. Du Charme. You said she is quite the lady. Coming up the stairs, I studied that portrait of her and the general. She is attractive."

"In her own way," he answered.

"She has allowed us to use this lovely villa and provided us with carefree days by leaving Celeste and Claude to wait on all of us. What does she expect in return?"

His clear blue eyes sparkled. "Why Mrs. Burke, do I detect a tad of jealousy?"

"It has crossed my mind, more than once, that you may get lonely, and the women around here may get lonely, and that loneliness could easily lead to temptations thrown in your path."

He slowly nodded his head as though con-templating that possibility. "That is something to think about. In fact, yielding to temptation doesn't sound like a bad idea."

She playfully tapped him on the chest. "Now you are teasing me."

"Of course I am. Rest assured, you are the only woman I can handle. Besides, I'm so worn out working at the hospital, all I can do is fall into bed until it's time to get up and start all over again."

She kissed his cheek and snuggled closer. "That does give me some consolation. I can't wait until you come back home. Until then, I believe we can spare a few wanton minutes in this bed."

"You are also a mind reader."

Thirty minutes later they were looking over the balcony railing into the large living area. It was alive with the sounds of the children who had opened presents. Ann Catherine was dragging a rag doll that Asa had given her while Matthew was trying to hit a ball with a paddle.

Catherine leaned over the rail. "Good morning," she called.

"There are the late risers," said Carolyn. "We've waited breakfast and we're starved."

"How could you be starved after that grand feast of last evening?" asked Catherine. "Let's call Celeste and Claude in and give them their presents."

She and Patrick hurried down the stairs.

"First, you ladies must open yours," ordered Andrew. "Where is Mattie?"

"She's still in her room," replied Elizabeth.

"That won't do. She has a gift to open."

"Patrick," said Catherine. "You go up and ask her to come down. She won't refuse you."

These three grown men were more excited than the children. The women looked at each other with questioning looks. It appeared their husbands had taken it upon themselves to do their own shopping.

When Mattie arrived, Patrick seated her next to Catherine. Each woman was presented

171

a colorfully decorated gift wrapped in red satin ribbon.

"One, two, three! Open!" said Andrew.

Without hesitation, they tore off the ribbons and unwrapped the gifts. The women exclaimed in oohs and aahs when they saw what the boxes contained.

Elizabeth received a string of pearls, which Andrew fastened around her slender neck.

Carolyn held up a filigree necklace sporting rubies. "Asa, it is beautiful."

"May I do the honor?" he asked as he stepped forward and kissed her cheek before clasping the necklace.

Catherine's present was a gold necklace inlaid with emeralds. She was choked with emotion when Patrick fastened the chain.

Mattie waffled between joy and embarrassment. Her gift was a silver pocket watch. She pushed a button and jumped when the cover flipped up.

"We wound it up and set it for you, Mattie, so the watch is ready to use," advised Patrick.

For the first time Catherine could remember, that giant of a woman was close to tears. After turning the watch this way and that and fingering the raised design of a flower on the lid, she regained her composure. "I ain't never had anythin' so grand. Why, Miz' Catherine I can carry this in my apron pocket and never have to run to that big clock in the hall."

"I believe the gentlemen have astounded all of us," Catherine answered.

Asa sprang from Carolyn's side. "Come on, Andrew. Let's round up our help."

They returned a few minutes later with a reluctant Celeste and Claude, who dutifully came but stood apart from the group that was gathered.

Elizabeth went to greet them and addressed them in French. Still reluctant, they sidled into the room to the nearest chairs.

Elizabeth presented the women's gifts first. The joyous look on Celeste's face told that she was more than pleased with the perfume, and Claude grinned from ear to ear as he tried on the new fine leather gloves.

Patrick brought the gifts the men had picked out. For Celeste, a box of chocolates, for Claude, a bottle of brandy. The candy brought a smile, the brandy brought a grimace from Celeste and a grin from Claude.

The French maid addressed Elizabeth before she and Claude stood, bowed to those present and left the room.

"She wants us to know that we have been pleasant house guests, which isn't always what they experience. She and Claude appreciate the gifts and they wish us all a safe journey home."

What had the women procured for their men?

"I think I speak for all three of us when I say you left us flabbergasted," said Catherine. "We offer: wine, cheese, crackers, sausages, dried fruit

173

and nuts." She pulled a white linen cover from a red wicker basket to reveal its contents.

A card was attached: *To our dear husbands: Although this is a very special Christmas we will always remember, may our next Christmas be spent in the good old USA. Our love, Catherine, Carolyn and Elizabeth*

"I believe you forgot the best gift of all. Your decision to come to France," said Asa. "You three deserve a medal for courage."

Celeste rang the bell announcing breakfast.

"What do you say, gentlemen? Shall we escort these brave lasses to the dining room?"

Arm in arm they headed to where Mattie and the children waited.

"I can't believe this will be our last day together. We should say a prayer of thanksgiving. Who would like to offer?" asked Elizabeth.

They looked at each other.

Mattie took up the cause. "Lord Almighty, we are thankful fer these men and women, these sweet children an' fer the use of this lovely house. As you give us a safe trip over here, we ask fer a safe trip home. Fer Major Thomas an' Major Caldwell, we pray you will guard them through this war. Fer Mistah Patrick, give him strength to do his doctorin'. We thank you fer this food an' ask yer blessin' on all of us here. Amen."

"Amen," came a chorus of replies.

"Mattie, that was a touching prayer. Thank you," said Catherine.

"Well, no one was jumpin' in an' our food was gettin' cold."

They shared a laugh, then ate with hearty appetites.

Celeste and Claude were leaving after breakfast to spend the day with relatives. When she relayed that information to Elizabeth, she also acknowledged that Claude was her son.

It didn't come as much of a surprise. The men had surmised that only a son would stand for Celeste's bossy ordering about.

Once again Mattie took charge of the children so the three couples could spend the day together.

The six of them cleaned up the remainder of the gift wrappings and undecorated the little Christmas tree that had given them such pleasure.

They retired to their rooms and the women began packing for the trip back home.

Patrick rested on the bed.

"Patrick, do you think it was foolhardy for me to spend the money for these short days? I've tried to be frugal since I closed the shop. This war may last for years."

"If I thought it was a mistake, I would have said so when you told me your plan. I have missed you, Catherine. You are not to worry about money. I still own ten percent of my brother's import business. He has a contract with the Army which is making him a lot of money."

She turned and smiled at him. "I will count every day until you arrive on our doorstep in April.

In the meantime, this packing can wait." She walked to where he rested. "I believe you and I have more important activities to fill our time."

How lucky he was to have snagged this woman he adored.

Across the way, Asa was helping Carolyn gather her belongings together.

"Shouldn't you be resting while you have the chance?" asked Carolyn.

"How can I rest when all I want to do is feast my eyes on you?"

She kissed the cheek of her robust cavalry major. "Asa, I don't know what I would do if something happened to you."

He encircled her in the security of his arms. "It's not like you to worry. What brought this on?"

The strength emanating from him was her comfort. "It's silly of me, but after seeing all of these preparations, going down into that trench and touring the hospital I realized the dangers. Viewing this war at a distance is much easier than seeing the reality close up."

"Do you think it was a mistake to come?"

She turned around to face him. "Oh, never. I wouldn't have missed these days with you for anything."

"That sounds more like my wife," he responded and kissed her soundly. "I will promise to do my best to keep out of harm's way."

She left his side and folded some clothes into a pile.

Asa stood looking out the window. "Patrick said he is planning on going home in April," he said. "If he does, he can help you three ladies out if the need arises. I know Andrew and I would be more comfortable knowing you had someone to rely on."

She stopped and looked at him. "We three women are good at relying on each other. Are you saying that you will not be coming back home after the six months is up?"

"I'm saying no one knows how involved we will be in this war. If we are extended, it will ease our minds to know Patrick is available. Now, what do you say to leaving this packing business and enjoying our last day together?"

She laughed, dropped the clothes in her hands and went to him. Winding her arms around his neck, she twirled her fingers in his coal black hair.

In one swoop, he picked her up and headed for the bed. "Let's pretend this is our second honeymoon."

"My very thought," she agreed.

Would this be their last time together?

In the next room, Andrew was pensive as he lounged on the bed and watched with admiration as Elizabeth meticulously prepared items to pack in her suitcase.

"Perhaps we should have waited to be married."

She turned with a start. "Are you unhappy?"

He was off the bed in an instant. "Of course not. You are my life. But I feel that I haven't been fair to you. I almost pushed you into marriage. Then I promised you a house on the base. That didn't happen and now you're stuck with your parents. Then this war came between us…"

She put a finger to his lips. "Hush, Andrew. I am right where I want to be. As long as I have you and Matthew, I can weather any storm."

Andrew's smile always lit up his handsome face. "He is a joy and I'm glad you are not alone. When I get home I will make it all up to both of you."

"After coming here, I doubt you will be back with us when your six months is up."

He drew her over to the bed where they sat on the edge holding hands. "I can't say for sure. We came over to set up the headquarters, which is almost finished, but there is nothing that says we will be shipped home when that is completed."

"Andrew, let's forget about the war, the headquarters, the training and all that goes with it. Let's concentrate on the few hours we have left and make the most of them. I've seen how the French women send flirtatious looks in your direction. I'm going to leave you with memories that will transcend all enticements."

"Elizabeth, I set my cap for you the first day we met under the oak tree on the Mitchell estate. There is not another woman who could turn my head, and I've had my pick of the crop. I keep my hope alive that I will only be here a few more months."

They wrapped together in each other's arms and forgot the world around them, hoping the future would be theirs.

Chapter 19

Claude took those leaving on the ocean liner to the harbor at Brest. He was always proud to drive in the carriage from the villa.

The whole area was abuzz with sailors, soldiers and dock workers. An Army band played patriotic music as huge tanks and large guns were wheeled off carriers.

The HMT Czar sat waiting. This was the same ship that brought the women to France.

Patrick was there on the dock when they arrived. He was the only husband who could get the time away.

The women shared hugs and tears with both Patrick and Claude as they bid goodbye. They waved from the deck of the ship as the ocean liner backed away from the wharf.

After the boat left the harbor, Patrick and a French doctor were to examine Claude. Patrick had already determined the young man had one leg shorter than the other. They would explain this condition to him and have a special shoe made with a lift. If it worked properly, the extra height would help straighten his posture and allow him to walk with less of a limp.

Claude drove Patrick up to the hospital where a teen-aged boy was paid to watch the carriage. The two men entered through the curved stone entrance of the large former nunnery.

Patrick led Claude to a small office where his colleague was waiting. Once the French physician explained the process, Claude grinned from ear to ear. He asked if he could join the army once the shoe was fitted. The doctor sidestepped the issue by saying that would be up to the French officers. The likelihood was slim.

That afternoon Patrick was signaled that he had a visitor. He left the floor of the hospital where he was working and went to the administration area.

There, dressed in a sable coat and exquisite velvet hat, stood Madeline DuCharme.

"Mrs. Du Charme. This is an unexpected pleasure," Patrick greeted her and guided her to a private alcove containing two chairs. They sat facing each other.

"How nice to see you Doctor Burke. I just arrived from England and wanted to be sure all went well at the villa."

"Yes, we were pleased," Patrick answered. "We would like to compensate you for the use of your home. It was far above our expectations."

She leaned closer and touched his arm. "Oh indeed not. It was the least I could do after you treated my little one."

Patrick was uncomfortable with her familiarity. "My wife and our friends were thankful. We lacked for nothing. In fact, Claude drove the ladies to the ship this morning. Another doctor and

I are having a special shoe made for him to ease his posture."

"That's wonderful. I hope it doesn't allow him such freedom that he will want to leave his position at the villa."

"You will have to discuss that with him."

She placed both hands over his. "Of course. I'm sure it will take some time to fit the shoe when it is ready. I will be happy to accompany him. Perhaps you and I might have tea together."

"I seldom have time to get away from my duties."

"But, you must take time. I'm sure you've heard that old proverb "all work and no play makes a dull person" or something similar to those words." Her laugh was delicate. She lifted her hands from his much to Patrick's relief. "I will be on my way. I am delighted you enjoyed the house."

Patrick watched her leave before he started off to his work. She was a striking woman.

Walking through the hall, he rubbed the back of his neck. Was it weariness or confusion? It was late afternoon on the 26th of December. He had seen his wife off on her voyage just this morning. Why did it seem like days ago?

The ward was bustling when he returned.

"Dr. Burke, we have fifteen more cases of Spanish flu," said a nurse. "I have put them together with the others but the space is getting cramped."

Patrick shook his head in dismay. "We're getting more soldiers with the flu than with war injuries. I'll speak to the head physician to see if we can isolate them on one wing of the hospital. We might need the whole floor if this keeps up. I prefer to have them away from the other patients."

Another nurse came up to him. "Dr. Burke, do you have time to see this English soldier in the third bed? His dressings smell of infection and he has started running a fever. His condition has deteriorated since this morning."

Patrick followed her to the bedside where he removed the bandages from the wound. The putrid smell was overpowering. Green bubbly discharge was draining from the area. The nurse and doctor looked at each other. They had seen cases of gas gangrene too frequently. Any treatment was unlikely to stem the course of this condition.

"Be sure and wrap those soiled bandages to be burned. I'll write orders for medicine to keep him as comfortable as possible."

"Yes, sir," she replied and hurried off to get supplies.

Patrick had no sooner left the bedside when he was asked to assist a surgeon with a foot amputation.

By ten o'clock that night he had picked up a sandwich from a Red Cross cart and ate it on the way to his dimly lit room. He peeled off his clothes and fell onto the cot in his underwear. It had been an exhausting day, as were most of the days he spent. The few days he'd been with Catherine were the first relaxing days he'd had since he arrived in October. It was no wonder she was concerned about the weight he had lost. He knew he couldn't keep

183

up this pace forever, which strengthened his vow to return to Washington in April. If I last that long, he thought.

Four days later, Claude returned for his appointment for fitting the shoe. Although he came alone, he carried a note to Patrick from his employer:

Dear Dr. Burke,

    I am hosting a party at the villa on December 31st to celebrate the beginning of a new year. There will be dinner and music and delightful company to relieve our cares and worries of the day.

    Please come and join us. I will send Claude for you at six o'clock on that evening.

    You must not disappoint those who would like to meet you.

                    Sincerely,
                    Madeline

Patrick's first inclination was to send a polite note declining the invitation. The more he thought about it the more appealing it sounded to get away from the hospital and enjoy an evening of dinner and music. Perhaps General Du Charme would be there and he would have the chance to meet him. So, he changed his mind and sent a reply of acceptance by way of Claude, who was trying to get used to the platform shoe by walking to and fro in the small room.

Satisfied with the way the shoe improved his appearance, Claude kissed the doctors on both cheeks, stuffed Patrick's note into his coat pocket and clunked out the door.

On New Year's Eve Patrick dressed in his best black suit, white shirt and black tie. The suit pants were a little big so he punched another hole in his belt to make them tighter. A pair of suspenders would have helped.

At six o'clock he was standing at the door of the hospital when Claude came by with a two seat buggy. Patrick wore an overcoat, gloves and wool hat. A fur robe in the buggy covered their laps to make a pleasant ride the mile and a half to the villa.

Madeline Du Charme met him at the door. Her silken strawberry-colored hair was wrapped in a fashionable twist. Her evening dress was gold satin with touches of fine lace over the bodice and at the plunging v-neckline. There was no mistaking the dress was made to accentuate her inviting figure. A strand of pearls and expensive pearl earrings completed her outfit.

She took Patrick's hand. "I am so pleased you could come."

A maid he had not seen before took his coat, hat and gloves.

"You must come and meet my guests."

The living room was alive with small gatherings of people all sipping wine. A trio of musicians played soothing music in one corner of the vast room.

185

Patrick glanced about and was quick to pick up on the superficiality of those present. It seemed no different than a Washington dinner party. He counted sixteen male and female guests in all, suspecting they were: politicians, bankers, businessmen, lawyers. Apparently, all making money off the war without having to be near the battle zones. Unless he was in civilian garb, there was no General Du Charme.

Madeline introduced him as the American doctor who saved her child. Patrick was embarrassed and would have protested if it would have done any good. He knew this engaging woman was enjoying her role. It would be impolite to usurp the attention she seemed to relish. It also allowed her to hold onto Patrick.

At dinner he was seated at her right.

The man across the way had a bit too much wine. To Madeline he said, "You look ravishing tonight. It's a shame your husband can't be here to appreciate your charms. I am always available." Then he guffawed.

Madeline took it in stride. "Chauncey, you must behave yourself. You will make Dr. Burke uncomfortable."

She reached over and pressed Patrick's arm. "You will have to forgive Chauncey. He is a dear friend."

Patrick wondered how dear. This behavior was not to his liking, and he wished he had never consented to come.

When dinner was over they returned to the living room where the band had increased the tempo of the music they were playing.

The leader announced the group would play two American songs for the American doctor. The first was George M. Cohan's, "You're a Grand Old Flag". The next was Cole Porter's, "If You Were the Only Girl in the World".

"I believe we could dance to that one," suggested Madeline as she led Patrick to the middle of the room.

A few other couples had decided the same thing.

She settled herself into his arms so their bodies were touching, the smoothness of her cheek resting on his. "I do admire you, Patrick," she whispered in his ear. "Why don't you spend the night here so you can get some rest before you have to face the hospital tomorrow?"

The woman was far too enticing. A surge of heat spread through his body as he danced her around the floor. Perhaps a night in a comfortable bed would do no harm. Suddenly, a vision of Catherine flashed through his mind. Clear your head, Patrick!

When the song was over, he addressed the woman who had almost made him forget who he was. "Thank you for a lovely evening, Mrs. Du Charme, but I must be getting back. I wish you a promising new year ahead."

She slipped her arm through his. "But, you must not go. Stay with me and we will forget all of this torment of war around us."

"Mrs. Du Charme, you have a husband in Paris, and I have a wife, whom I love, heading back to America. I will say good night."

At the door she gave him a passionate kiss. "Are you sure you don't want to stay?"

The woman was tenacious. He needed to leave. "I am sure."

A heavy sigh escaped her lips. "I will have Celeste tell Claude to drive you back."

"It is only a mile and a half. The moon is full and the cold air will open my senses. Good bye, Mrs. Du Charme."

She turned and left him at the door. As he was leaving, he heard her delicate laugh followed by, "Oh, Chauncey. You are such a devil."

Chapter 20

When the HMT Czar docked at Hoboken, New Jersey on the morning of January 4th, 1918, Catherine, Carolyn and Elizabeth were grateful to be back in the United States of America. Although the weather wasn't any cheerier than what they had experienced in France, and the accents of the people they encountered were different than their native Virginian, it was American soil and they felt at home.

There was an array of vehicles lined up to take passengers to their next stop. The women spied a conveyance that looked much like the twelve passenger car Herbert Marks used to drive to the Bluemont station.

"Let's ask the driver if he can take us to Grand Central Terminal in New York City," suggested Catherine.

"How much do you think it will cost?" asked Carolyn. "I'm getting close with the money I brought, and we still have to buy train tickets and get home from Union Station once we get back to Washington."

"Elizabeth," said Catherine. "Go ask the man what he will charge to drive us."

"Why do I have to go?"

"Because you will get the best price. All you have to do is look at a man and he is ready to do your bidding," replied Carolyn.

Elizabeth grimaced and heaved a sigh. "Well, I don't know why either of you can't do the same thing."

"Because we don't have blonde hair, blue eyes and get men's heads to turn like you do," answered Catherine.

Meanwhile, the children were getting restless and Mattie was beginning to chafe at the bit. "If'n somebody don' do somethin', we gonna' stand on these wet boards and catch our death o'cold."

"I'm on my way," said a chagrined Elizabeth.

They stood and watched as she approached the man and pleaded her case. He doffed his cap, offered a smile in the ladies' direction and winked at Elizabeth before she turned to walk back to the group.

"I hope you're satisfied. He said he usually charges fifty cents a mile and fifty cents for each extra passenger. He will take us for half price and no charge for the children if they sit on our laps."

"How do we know that's a good price?" asked Carolyn.

"Take it or leave it," was Elizabeth's exasperated answer. "It's about five miles to the station. I figure if we three put in a dollar and a half each that will pay for the fare and give him a generous gratuity."

"Done," said Catherine.

They settled into the car while the driver piled in the luggage.

A well-dressed couple walked to the long car. "We understand you are on your way to Grand Central Terminal," said the man. "Do you have room for two more?"

"Room toward the back," answered the driver, motioning with his thumb.

"How much is the fare?"

"Fifty cents a mile and fifty cents for each extra passenger."

"Outrageous!" exclaimed the man.

"We have little choice," said his wife.

The driver hefted their suitcases, while the two entered the car to take seats.

"Prices keep going up," grumbled the man on his way to the back seat. "Unions will put this country under. You mark my words."

"Yes, dear," came the wife's tired reply.

Elizabeth nudged Carolyn. "Did you hear the price he told them?" she whispered. "He's being generous to us."

"See?" Carolyn whispered back. "I told you the men can't resist you."

Elizabeth shook her head and chuckled.

Catherine leaned her head in and asked in a quiet voice, "Do you think the driver is Italian?"

Carolyn and Elizabeth sent quizzical looks to each other and shrugged their shoulders.

"What difference does it make?" questioned Elizabeth.

"I hear there are a lot of Italians in New York, and I don't know if he is speaking with an Italian accent or if that's the way all the people around here talk."

"As long as he knows where he's going, I don't care if he's German. Honestly, Catherine. I don't understand you," said Carolyn.

"From what I've heard, the Italian men like to pinch a woman's derriere. I want to be prepared."

Elizabeth and Carolyn laughed out loud.

"I don't think you'd feel a thing through that fancy corset you're wearing," Carolyn said and fell back into laughter.

The tall driver was rather good-looking with black wavy hair, a well-trimmed mustache, smooth olive complexion, laughing dark eyes and an alluring smile. He had a certain flair as he moved about.

"You ladies are having too much fun back there," he called from the driver's seat. "How about letting me in on it?"

"I do believe we are giddy from our trip to France," came Carolyn's quick answer.

"You've got to watch out for those Frenchmen, or so I've heard," he replied, with a good-natured chortle.

Catherine turned a delicate pink. "I hope he didn't hear me."

Carolyn waved away the thought. She raised her voice and asked, "Will it take long before we reach the terminal?"

"I'll have you there in half-an-hour if the traffic isn't heavy."

"Thank you," said Carolyn. "We are all eager to get back to Washington."

"I'm sure you are," he replied. "Too bad you can't stay around. New York City has a lot to offer."

"One day, when this war is over, we hope to explore it with our husbands."

"All the good-lookin' ones are married," came the driver's lament.

Grand Central Terminal loomed before them as the long car made its way down forty-second street. The massive granite building had giant clock towers on each corner of the roof.

"There used to be twelve cast iron eagles on the old station before they tore it down," informed the driver. "Each one had a wing span of fourteen feet and each weighed over four thousand pounds. They were scary-looking devils. Had mouths wide open like they were going to swoop down and carry you off. This new terminal is a beauty, covers acres." He pulled the car to a halt at the curb. "Here we are ladies, last stop before you head for Washington."

Inside the vast, ornate terminal the small band crowded together lest they get swept away into the throngs of people.

"All of you wait here," ordered Catherine, "while I purchase the tickets."

Without waiting for a reply she strode to a window with a lighted ticket sign above it. "I need four tickets on the next train leaving for Washington.

We also have two little ones. Is there a charge for them?"

"Can they sit on your laps?"

"Yes."

"Then they won't cost a thing, lady. We only charge for those taking up seats. According to this schedule," he said, looking at a chalkboard behind him, "the next train out of here is due to leave in one hour. You can board it on the southbound track platform. Track 2."

"What about our luggage?"

"Have a porter wheel it down to the platform. They'll mark it and load it there."

"The porter knows how to get to the right track?"

The ticket agent laughed. "If he don't, he ain't got no business working here."

"Thank you," she replied and placed the tickets in her pocketbook.

She addressed those waiting, "We have to find a porter to wheel our luggage to the right place. The train leaves in an hour."

"We're lucky," said a relieved Elizabeth. "I thought we might be stuck here for hours."

A small group of porters were talking and laughing together a short distance from where the women waited. They waved and motioned to the men, who looked their way but paid no attention.

Without a word, Mattie, who held a squirming Matthew, left her seat and walked to where three colored men, wearing round red hats strapped under their chins and black uniforms, were talking.

The women watched as Mattie marched up to them, gestured with an arm, nodded her head with authority and left with one of the men following her.

She stood guard as the short man loaded the luggage on a cart. "Now, Miz' Catherine. You tell this man where we needs to go."

"Southbound platform to get a train to Washington."

"Yes, ma'am. You jus' follow me."

The little group traipsed behind the porter wheeling the load of luggage to the southbound platform that was on the same level but a good distance away and outside of the main terminal.

"Why did the other porters ignore us?" Catherine asked Mattie as they walked along.

"Becuz' they's lazy an' they didn't think they'd get a good tip from women."

"I suspected as much. How did you get them to move?"

"I tol' 'em yer husband's a general and he'd have their sorry behinds over in the war if'n one o' them didn't help."

Catherine chuckled. "You do know how to get things done."

It was twenty minutes later when they reached their destination. Catherine collected money from Carolyn and Elizabeth.

She smiled as she handed the porter seventy-five cents, a generous tip. "Be sure and tell your

195

friends, who ignored us, they missed their chance. Perhaps the next time they won't be so selective."

A faint apologetic look appeared on his face before he grinned and shoved the gratuity into his pocket.

The women found a place to sit inside a windowed room where they could watch the trains as they came and went. It was quieter than standing on the platform, but still noisy, and the room shook with the movement of each train.

"I am exhausted," said Elizabeth. "Mattie, I am so happy to have your help with Matthew."

He was now asleep on the big woman's shoulder.

"Miz' Elizabeth, I done seen he be a han'ful fer you, but he's a sweet baby. It jus' takes more to keep up with a boy than it does with a girl. An' I 'spect it ain't easy fer you to be livin' with yer parents. Mebbe' I shouldn't say this, but I 'spect yer momma still bosses you aroun'. That might be troublin' fer Matthew to figger' out who he needs to listen to."

Elizabeth looked at her with big eyes. "Mattie, I think you're right. If it was just Matthew and me together, he would listen to me better."

"Leastwise, that's how I sees it."

The Washington train was on time. The women gathered up their bags and settled into the passenger car. The little ones were worn out and stayed asleep even with all the maneuvering to get onto the train.

"I will be so glad to get back to Washington," offered Carolyn. "We have been in a whirlwind for three weeks."

"I thought you were the one who liked adventure," said Catherine.

Carolyn yawned. "I'm beginning to think I prefer it in small doses."

"When we get to Union Station, why don't you both bring the children to my house and spend the night? We can drop Mattie off on the way and none of us will have to go home by ourselves."

"That sounds good to me," answered Carolyn. "How about you Elizabeth?"

"Count me in. It'll be late and my mother would probably be disgruntled if I woke them up."

"You need to do something about that situation," advised Carolyn.

"I'm thinking about it," Elizabeth replied.

They all leaned back with a relaxed sigh.

"Once we get to Washington, I'll buy some breakfast foods," said Catherine.

"I'm all for it," answered an enthused Carolyn.

Chapter 21

The Burke house in Georgetown was alive with the sounds of morning by the time they all arose. Catherine had percolated coffee and was frying ham. The biscuits were browning.

Carolyn and Elizabeth had dressed the children and they were sitting at the table eating pancakes without syrup.

"Carolyn, if you'll scramble the eggs, we can all sit down and eat. I'm hungry," said Catherine.

"Elizabeth, you keep an eye on Annie, it won't take but a couple of minutes for me to fix the eggs. I feel like I haven't eaten in a week."

When all was ready, Catherine placed the biscuits on the table, dished up the eggs and ham while Carolyn poured coffee.

"Elizabeth, do you want me to put some scrambled eggs on the children's plates?" asked Catherine.

"That will be good. They'll also eat some ham. I'll cut it up for them."

The little group sat at the table while they ate and savored the warm coffee.

"This isn't as grand as the villa, but I'm glad to be back," surmised Catherine.

The others nodded.

"It was good to be waited on, though, wasn't it?" said Carolyn. "I've never had that luxury."

Elizabeth rubbed the side of her cup. "Andrew encouraged me to stay at Red Gate Farm until he returns. I've been giving it a lot of thought."

Carolyn was quick with her reply, "I think you should."

"It would mean getting his parents' permission," she mused.

"I'm sure Mr. Caldwell will be overjoyed to have you and Matthew there. I can't think of a better way for them to get acquainted with their grandson. Emily was all for it."

Elizabeth smiled at the thought. "You're probably right. You know the family better than I do. One thing I do know is that I don't want to stay at my parents' house any longer."

Catherine sat listening. "Elizabeth, I think you are wise to consider the change. Andrew wouldn't have suggested it unless he thought it would be best for the two of you."

"My goodness, look at the time," exclaimed Carolyn. "I need to get back and make sure the house at the base is just as I left it." She started to clear the table.

"Leave it where it is," ordered Catherine. "It will give me something to do once you're gone."

"That sounds good to me," said Carolyn. "Come on, Annie. Mommy's going to get you ready to go home."

**

Carolyn arrived at the base in mid-morning. She took her suitcase up the front stairs to the porch and left it by the door. "We're going to walk to the post office and see if we have a letter from your daddy," she said to Annie.

There were patches of snow on the ground, but the winter sun was peeking through low clouds making a cheerier walk.

They stopped at the commissary where Carolyn bought milk and bread. She knew there would still be oatmeal, peanut butter and jelly at the house. Other groceries could wait until they were settled and after she made a list.

At the post office, she was disappointed to find the box empty.

They passed the parade grounds where soldiers on horseback were in dress uniforms drilling their horses into formations. How proud they looked. How unlikely any of this would be useful if they were sent to Europe.

Annie pointed. "Daddy," she said.

"No, sweetie. I wish it was. Daddy isn't here." An uncomfortable cold feeling came over her as she remembered the sights she had seen in France: the broken men in the hospital, the barren training grounds, the tomb-like trenches. Those sights had become Asa's world. The thought made her shiver.

Inside the house was cold. Carolyn set a fire in the fireplace while Annie found her doll in its little wicker carriage, which she proceeded to push around the room.

Coming home to the quiet house was such a let-down that Carolyn had to fight back tears. The hollow feeling hit with an unexpected force.

She wasn't going to shed tears in front of her child so she lugged in the suitcase and busied herself with sorting its contents. There was plenty to keep her busy.

Perhaps tomorrow would be a better day.

**

In Alexandria, Elizabeth was in the kitchen talking to the maid. Matthew was pulling a wooden train across the wood floor.

"Train. See Mommy?"

"Yes, I see and I hear it."

She said to Opal, "I'd better find him something quiet to play with before Mother hears the racket."

Too late. The door opened. "What is that awful noise?" came her mother's annoyed request.

"I'm sorry, Mother. I was about to find him something less noisy."

"My goodness, I hope so. That sound echoes all over the house. Matthew, you are giving your grandmother a headache."

Elizabeth sighed. "I'll take him out for a walk."

"Don't be out for long. Your father is taking us to the Willard for lunch. Leave Matthew with Opal."

"Mother, I'm tired from the trip. I don't care to go to lunch. When I put Matthew down for a nap, I'll take one also."

Gertrude Fairchilds wagged her head. "You have no choice. Your father and I want to hear about your visit to France." She turned and left the room.

Elizabeth knew trying to change her mother's mind would only cause consternation.

"Opal, I am going to send a letter to Andrew's parents and ask if Matthew and I can stay there until he returns."

"If you think that's best," replied the maid.

"Mother and I seem to be at odds on every-thing. She is still trying to run my life."

"You're her only child and she doesn't know how to let go. If you and the little one would be happy out there, you ought to make the change."

Elizabeth was dressing Andrew to go outdoors. "I don't know if I'd be any happier. I don't like to be away from the city. On the other hand, I don't want to be cooped up in the apartment over the hat shop in Berryville. I know I'll say words I'll regret if I stay here."

"Then it looks like you got no choice."

Elizabeth kissed her cheek. "Thanks, Opal. I guess I just needed one more person to tell me that. It will only be until Andrew gets back."

"Miz' Elizabeth, don't you fret. It will all work out."

"One way or another," she replied with a half-smile.

**

Catherine Burke was cleaning up the kitchen when Mattie came in the back door.

"I'm glad you're here," Catherine greeted her. "I'm sure Jacob was pleased to have you back safe and sound."

Mattie took off her hat and hung up her coat. "He wanted to hear all about it. Seems we talked half the night."

"You should have stayed home today to rest up. Carolyn, Elizabeth and the children left a couple of hours ago."

"I know you done gots clothes to wash and things to put away. An' this house ain't bin dusted fer three weeks."

"Mattie, I think I am going to volunteer with the Red Cross."

"What's that?"

"They help in the war effort. That can be my contribution until Patrick gets home in April. It will keep me busy."

"Seein' you ain't runnin' the hat shop, I guess you needs somethin' to keep you goin'."

"I couldn't have put it in better terms. I guess I might as well unpack that suitcase in the foyer. You heat the water for the tub. One of these days I'm going to have a copper washing machine like the one Elizabeth's parents own."

Mattie smiled. "Miz' Catherine, yer big wash tubs be fine with me. We'd best get started."

Chapter 22

Francis and Gertrude Fairchilds were taking Elizabeth and Matthew to the Alexandria train station. A truck had picked up the two trunks she had packed for the move to Red Gate Farm.

"I don't know why you are leaving us, Elizabeth," said her mother.

"I'm not leaving you. I am just going to stay at the farm until Andrew returns. It will give the Caldwells a chance to get better acquainted with Matthew."

"I don't understand it. Tearing yourself away from all the city has to offer to go live in the country, where there is nothing. And, after all we've done for you."

"Gertie," said Francis. "I understand. Elizabeth is a grown woman and can make her own decisions."

"Well, I wish someone could explain it to me," huffed the mother.

"I wish we could too," answered Francis, with a heavy sigh. "Elizabeth that looks like the truck you hired to bring your trunks. They're unloading them now." He pulled the Tin Lizzie into a place near the station.

Elizabeth carried one small satchel so she could keep hold of Matthew's hand. "Give Grandma and Grandpa a kiss. We're going to take a ride on the train."

"Train ride! Train ride!" shouted Matthew.

"Yes, your mother is dragging you off to the hinterlands," lamented Gertrude.

Matthew stood behind the front seat and Elizabeth held him up so he could kiss each of his grandparents.

"We're going to miss you, little man," said Francis and patted Matthew's cap.

"I promise to write. You know we are only going to be seventy miles away. You could come out to visit. You can stay in the apartment in town for a few days."

"I couldn't imagine having to walk up and down those stairs all the time," was her mother's reply.

Elizabeth didn't offer that they might stay at the farm.

She picked up her satchel off the floor of the car. "It's something to think about," she said. "In two months it will be spring and there is nothing prettier than the country in the spring."

Francis left the driver's seat and opened the back door. "We will certainly keep it in mind," said the peacemaker. He hugged his only child. "I hope this works out for you,"

"Thank you for all you and Mother have done. Once Andrew returns, all our lives will be settled down."

He gave her hand a gentle squeeze. "You hurry on now so you don't miss your train."

Elizabeth watched as they drove away. Gertrude held a hankie to her face. Could she be shedding a tear? No, thought Elizabeth, it's more likely she is shielding her nose from the odor emitting from the idling cars.

The train ride was tedious, especially with a twenty-two month old child. At every stop, she took him off the train so he could run a bit. In Leesburg, where there was a fifteen minute stopover, Elizabeth changed his diapers and washed his face and hands. There was just enough time to get drinks from the water fountain and buy cookies before it was time to start the next leg of the journey.

Matthew was content with the cookies. Elizabeth showed him a book with pictures of animals and, after turning a few pages, he fell asleep. She looked at the watch that hung from a chain around her neck. With luck, her handsome little boy would nap until they reached Bluemont.

Stuart and a hired hand from the farm were waiting with a carriage. "We'll tie those trunks on the back and the four of us will ride up front," Stuart said. "We knew people and belongings weren't going to fit in the touring car, although I'd rather drive that than this carriage."

He didn't introduce the colored man with him.

Elizabeth turned to him. "What is your name?" she asked.

He inclined his head and gave a wide smile. "Toby, ma'am."

"Of course, I should have realized. Miss Carolyn has spoken kindly of you. You are Ollie's husband."

"Yes, ma'am," he replied.

"Toby, get back here and help me load these trunks," ordered Stuart.

There was something about Stuart Elizabeth didn't like. She couldn't put her finger on the reason, but she had taken an instant dislike to the little man on her last visit to Red Gate.

The long ride to the farm was a quiet trip. Neither the driver nor his companion spoke, which Elizabeth thought unusual as the men worked at the same place. It seemed they could at least have inane topics to discuss. Perhaps there was a mutual dislike between the two men.

She had too much on her mind to be concerned with trivial matters.

When they reached the estate, Emily came out onto the elevated porch as the carriage drove up the tree-lined drive. She hurried down the long set of stone steps to help Elizabeth.

With a welcome hug, she said, "I am so glad you're here. Father Caldwell is waiting inside. Stuart, you and Toby see that Mrs. Caldwell's trunks get up to her quarters."

"Yes, ma'am," answered Toby. Stuart did not reply.

Emily kissed Matthew's cheek. "Matthew, were you a big boy and helped Mommy on the train?"

Just then a big spotted cat ran across the yard and under the porch. Matthew wiggled out of his mother's grasp intent on following it.

He wasn't fast enough. "Oh no you don't. Your suit was dirty the last time we came. I want Andrew's parents to see you neat and tidy," admonished his mother.

They started up the steps.

"His grandparents won't care," said Emily. "You had better get used to calling them Father and Mother Caldwell. They expect it."

"How is Andrew's mother?" asked Elizabeth.

"Not well. I see her daily so it may be more difficult to notice small changes. You haven't seen her in a few months. I believe you will be a better judge of her condition."

That wasn't news Elizabeth wanted to hear.

The first floor maid, Doris, took her coat and hat and waited while Elizabeth unbuttoned and removed Matthew's coat and cap.

"You may take them upstairs to Mr. Andrew's rooms," said Emily.

"Yes, ma'am," said Doris.

Elizabeth found her reception from the help much different than the way they had treated Carolyn.

"I don't think she likes me," whispered Elizabeth, after Doris went to the stairs.

"You have to give them time," answered Emily.

"Tell me about Stuart. I just don't care for him. I think he feels the same way toward me."

"Stuart takes a bit more of an explanation. We'll discuss him later. Now, we had better hurry to the parlor."

William Caldwell rose when they entered.

"Come in. Come in." He greeted them with a welcome smile. "Virginia, we have Andrew's wife and son visiting."

She raised her head as she sat in the wheelchair and offered a wan smile. It was obvious to Elizabeth that the woman did not recognize them.

She walked to where Virginia sat and took her frail hand in hers. "Mother Caldwell, it is good to be here. I have seen Andrew. He sends his love."

Virginia's reaction was a blank stare.

Emily brought Matthew to where Elizabeth stood. The visage of this woman in the wheelchair must have been too much for him because he let out a shriek and latched onto his mother burying his face in her skirt.

His reaction seemed to surprise everyone leaving Elizabeth embarrassed and at a loss for words.

William Caldwell stepped forward. "Elizabeth, bring him over here. I have a gift for him."

Elizabeth edged her way across the room, with Matthew clinging to her skirt, to where William Caldwell displayed a small metal object. A round body, with a long barrel protruding, sat on three wooden legs. William put a small wood pellet in the barrel, turned the crank, and the pellet shot out.

Matthew quickly forgot his upset and reached for the toy.

"We also found some old toys of Andrew's. You'll find them upstairs."

"Father Caldwell, I'm hoping he isn't going to be too noisy for you. Even with your letter of encouragement, I had reservations about coming."

"My dear," he said. "We need some noise in this all too quiet house. The offer would not have been extended if we had not wanted your company. This big house needs the spirit of youth. Now, you must both be tired. I am eager to hear your news of Andrew, which we will discuss at the dining table. Six o'clock."

Elizabeth smiled. "Yes, I remember," she said.

"I'll go upstairs with you," said Emily. "I have some paperwork to do before dinnertime."

A much relieved Elizabeth opened the door to Andrew's old quarters. It was the same as when they had shared them last July.

The larger of the two rooms held an iron bed covered by a white cotton bedspread with a patterned quilt laying across the foot of the bed.

Matthew's small cot was tucked into a corner of the room.

A stone fireplace warmed the interior. The ceiling was lower than the ones on the first floor giving the rooms a cozy feeling. There a dresser, wardrobe and writing desk. She opened the wardrobe to find some of Andrew's clothes hanging inside, and she was filled with the warmth of his presence.

The adjoining room was smaller but a perfect play area for Matthew. Windows in both rooms overlooked the rear lawn and Blue Ridge Mountains in the distance.

Any reservations she held dissipated in this comfortable place.

She did not have to unpack her trunks until tomorrow.

Matthew was busy building block towers giving Elizabeth time to write a letter to Andrew. The writing desk contained stationery and an ink pen.

Her hope was that the letter would reach him wherever he was. News had come in mid-January that the American troops were now fully entrenched in warfare.

Chapter 23

Carolyn Thomas was hanging clothes on the line while Ann Catherine was dragging a rag doll around the back yard of their house on the Army base.

Carolyn felt glum.

Elizabeth had left three weeks ago and Catherine was always busy helping with the Red Cross.

Carolyn had promised Asa that she wouldn't stay involved with the Suffragette Movement until he returned. He had heard about the night of terror in November when Suffragettes were brutally thrown in jail. Some women suffered life-threatening injuries and some, who refused to eat, were force-fed. 'When I return, we will discuss it further. I can't have your safety on my mind while I am over here. You must promise,' he had said.

Because she had to care for Ann Catherine, she couldn't work as a nurse or volunteer as Catherine did. The days were long and lonely.

The wind was chilly. If the sun was warm enough, it might dry the wet clothes or, at least, leave them damp so she could dry them near the fireplace.

The wind carried the voices of soldiers going through military drills and she thought about her Asa so far from home. She said a silent prayer that he was safe.

"Annie, it's getting cold out here. Let's you and Mommy go inside and have some warm milk."

Annie looked up and smiled at her mother. "Milk," she said.

Carolyn sat the laundry basket on the back stoop and picked up her daughter. "I wish your mommy was in a happier mood."

Ann Catherine kissed her mother's cheek as much as to say that she understood.

The mail arrived at naptime with a letter from Elizabeth. Carolyn settled Ann Catherine into her bed and brewed a cup of tea before she sat at the kitchen table to read it:

Dear Carolyn,

It is almost the end of February and I am looking forward to spring.

I trust all is well with you.

Catherine wrote that she is very busy helping the Red Cross with the war effort. It takes her mind off an empty house. She says she is waiting for that day in April when Patrick arrives.

For her sake, I hope it will come to pass.

As for our dear husbands, I know not where they are. Have you had any news about them? I do worry.

One of the reasons I am writing this letter is to tell you of Mrs. Caldwell's health. Her condition has deteriorated. She will soon be needing a nurse

213

to care for her, and I wondered if you might consider that position.

If you are open to the offer, I will talk with Father Caldwell. I am sure he would welcome having you caring for her once again. I fear that she will not recover.

You and Ann Catherine can stay at Red Gate, and I can watch her when you need to tend to Mother Caldwell's needs.

I believe I am finally accepted by the help. At least I am comfortable with them. They are good to Matthew and Father Caldwell takes him around the farm with him sometimes. In short, I am happy I came.

Oh, Carolyn, please say yes. You can't know how much I miss seeing you and Catherine.

Your forever friend,
Elizabeth

Yes, Elizabeth, I do know your feelings for I feel the same, thought Carolyn. She reread the letter with tears in her eyes. Was this opportunity the hand of Providence? Catherine would say it was.

There was no need to think it over. If Mr. Caldwell agreed to have her come and care for his wife, she would do so gladly. The letter lifted her spirits to a new high. She loved Red Gate Farm and the people there.

What more could she ask for than to be reunited with Elizabeth and to have Annie in her care? She would leave the confines of the Army base without reservations because the place only served to stir up memories of Asa.

Her search for adventure diminished after the trip to France. She would be content to use her nursing skills and be among those she held dear.

That evening she called Catherine to tell her of Elizabeth's letter. Catherine was not surprised about Virginia Caldwell's condition. Although she would miss Carolyn, she said it was a step that should be taken.

**

An early March day found Carolyn and her little daughter at the Alexandria station waiting for the train to Bluemont. She had packed one suitcase and a trunk. She smiled when the thought came to her about her first trip to Red Gate Farm from the Winchester Memorial Hospital Training School for Nurses. That time she had packed two apple crates and a small satchel. James Anderson, the self-assured handsome driver, had teased her, and she had brought him up short. At the memory, her smile widened. She always smiled at the thought of James.

Stuart and Toby met her at the Bluemont station with the Packard Touring car.

Carolyn greeted Toby with a hug.

"We figured you wouldn't be toting as much stuff as the other one so we didn't bring the carriage," said Stuart. "We can tie the trunk on the back."

"Are you referring to Mrs. Caldwell?" asked Carolyn, in a demanding tone.

"We had to tug two big trunks to the upper floor. About killed my back."

"Perhaps you should find a less strenuous position at another place," said Carolyn. "I will be happy to talk with Mr. Caldwell. He may know of someone looking for a driver."

Stuart didn't answer. "C'mon Toby, load this trunk."

It was easy to see why Elizabeth didn't like the cranky little man. There wasn't anything to like.

Even though it was March, the day was cold enough for a warm coat. On the way to the farm she saw budding trees and patches of green. They were probably weeds but any green was welcome after the bleakness of winter.

The stately manor house looked the same. As they drove up the tree-lined driveway, Stuart stopped in front of the porch steps. Toby hurried out of his seat to help Carolyn and Annie out of the back, then lifted her suitcase.

Carolyn stood and looked at the red brick manor house that held so many memories.

Elizabeth and Emily came out onto the porch. Elizabeth leaned over the wrought iron railing. "Carolyn, we have been waiting for you. You and Annie hurry on up here."

Carolyn did as she was bid leaving Stuart and Toby to cart in her belongings.

Elizabeth and Emily greeted her warmly. Ann Catherine clung to her mother's calf-length skirt.

Elizabeth crouched down to Annie's eye level. "Have you forgotten me? Matthew is playing inside. You can play with him if you want to."

Ann Catherine looked at her through wide dark eyes and inched even closer to her mother.

Elizabeth stood. "She's still the shy one, isn't she?"

"She'll be fine once she gets used to a new place."

"Well," Emily offered. "Come in out of the chill. Father Caldwell will want to see you and then we can all have a cup of hot tea."

William Caldwell was in his study. He stood when they entered. "Mrs. Thomas. How good of you to come. I see your little one has grown."

"Thank you, Mr. Caldwell. I wish I had come for a different reason, but I am glad that I can be of service. Elizabeth has informed me of Mrs. Caldwell's condition. Should I look in on her?"

"No. She's resting comfortably. You young ladies get settled. After dinner this evening you can start your care of Virginia. You will have your old room back."

"That's good to hear. It will be comfortable for us and easily accessible to your wife."

"Yes, I thought so. Now, you go ahead and freshen up. Those trains and rides down the mountain are tiresome. I trust there was no problem."

"None," answered Carolyn, keeping her displeasure with Stuart to herself.

The high-ceilinged room she had lived in when she nursed Virginia Caldwell a few years earlier looked the same: stone fireplace, four-poster cherry bed, cherry writing desk, blue embroidered settee, cherry dresser and pegs to hang her clothes. A cot had been added for Annie. How much her life had changed since she last occupied this room!

At dinner, Andrew's brother and sister joined them. Most conversation was about the trip to France. Near the end of the meal, Ruth thanked Carolyn for coming to care for her mother, which was the most civil she had ever been to Carolyn. Then she dropped the bombshell when she announced she would be traveling to England for an extended time.

This seemed to be news to the elder Caldwell. "Ruth, do you think that wise? Your mother is quite ill and may need you here."

"To do what, Father? Stand by and watch her die?"

"Ruth!" He slammed his fist on the table. "That kind of talk is uncalled for."

"I'm not sorry. She has gone downhill for the past couple of months. You have capable help to care for her and my presence isn't going to change anything. This may be an unfortunate time, but I have been invited to visit in England and I don't intend to let this opportunity slip by."

"Must be a well-heeled gentleman," chimed in her brother, Will. "You do realize there is a war going on. The Germans are said to have their submarines all over the ocean. Great Britain may be the next target."

"Nevertheless, I am determined to go."

"Pure folly," admonished the elder Caldwell.

"I am all packed and Stuart has orders to drive me to the Bluemont station. I am twenty-four years old and there is nothing you can do to change my mind. May I be excused?"

"And if I said no?"

"I'd excuse myself anyway."

Emily, Elizabeth and Carolyn sat in silence as this scene unfolded. They didn't dare look at each other.

Once Ruth left the room, William Caldwell spoke, shaking his head. "Strong-headed girl. Always has been. I'm going to ring for dessert. How are things going at the stables, Will?"

Now the three women looked at each other under raised eyelids. Was there no regret over Ruth's announced departure?

Chapter 24

By the time April arrived, those at Red Gate Farm had settled into a routine: Elizabeth was the caretaker for Ann Catherine and Matthew, Emily continued to teach in the makeshift school room in an old hop kiln and Carolyn attended to Virginia Caldwell, who was slowly wasting away. If she lived another month, Carolyn would be surprised.

The gloom of her frail condition that permeated the house was offset by the laughter and energy of Matthew and Annie. Was that the way God intended? One life passes and another takes its place?

News from France was that Asa and Andrew would not be coming home until the tide of war changed. They had spent the past months still in training and had yet to be engaged in combat on the Western Front. Although some of their men had been aiding in the war zone.

Their letters had been upbeat, but the women wondered if that was a façade for their true feelings. Surely, it must be difficult to go on from day to day not knowing what lay ahead.

The women had written back to tell Andrew of his mother's health and that Carolyn and Ann Catherine were now residing at Red Gate Farm.

Carolyn was glad that Ruth had left and Will was kept busy running the farm. They had been a thorn in her side when she last cared for Andrew's mother.

She and Elizabeth found time for tea when the little ones napped in the afternoons. It was a comfort for the two friends to be together.

On this day, when it was tea time, Elizabeth was excited as she placed a letter on the table. "It's from Catherine. Patrick is home! He arrived last week and they want to come out and visit."

Carolyn picked up the letter and read the news for herself. "Oh, Elizabeth, this will be wonderful. I have missed her these past few months. Although she has been steadfast in writing, it is not the same as having her here in person."

"Catherine asked if they could stay in town in the apartment. I have already penned a letter saying they are most welcome."

"Perhaps Patrick has news of our husbands since neither of us has had a letter for over two weeks. Have you written to Andrew about his mother's condition?"

Elizabeth poured another cup of tea. "Yes. I was honest and told him that she isn't expected to live. I didn't want to place a further burden on him, but he would want me to be truthful."

"And, well you should be. When do you think Catherine and Patrick will come?"

"I am assuming early in May. I should think Patrick needs some time to recover from his experience in France before he finds a place to set up his office."

"I can hardly wait to see them," said Carolyn. "Elizabeth you couldn't have brought any sunnier news. Now, I must get back to Mrs. Caldwell."

"How much longer do you expect?"

"She can still take water and the gruel Ollie mixes up. Once she can no longer take that it will be a matter of days."

"How do you think Father Caldwell will take it?"

"I believe he is already grieving. Sometimes death is easier to accept when you see loved ones fail day by day. When the time comes, it seems they are not the same person."

Elizabeth finished her tea. "When the children wake up from their naps, I am going to take them for a walk. I may stop by to see Emily." She leaned closer and whispered. "I think she has found an interest."

"Another shining pupil who shows a bud of intelligence?"

"No." She put a finger to her lips. "I think her interest is the strapping young man who works at the stables."

Carolyn's dark eyes opened wide. She whispered back. "Elizabeth, you shouldn't say that." Then just as quickly, "What makes you think so?"

"I've watched. She is always eager to go to the classroom. The others leave before he does. He always stays fifteen or twenty minutes later."

"Maybe that's why she's so cheery."

"Do you think I should say something?"

"Of course not."

"What if she gets found out?"

"That will be her problem. Will is so pompous and overbearing, perhaps she likes attention from someone else."

Elizabeth drew in her breath. "Carolyn, he's a hired man and she's a married woman!"

"Elizabeth, this will pass over so let her enjoy it while she can. Now, I must get back to your mother-in-law."

She rose from her chair, started for the door and whispered in Elizabeth's ear as she passed, "I'd stay away from the old hop kiln if I were you. Who knows what tawdry scene you may happen upon?"

**

Two weeks later, Catherine and Patrick arrived in a brand new four-door Maxwell automobile: red body, black fenders, yellow spoke wheels, windows around, and as high and square as the Model T.

Carolyn and Elizabeth watched from the porch as the newsworthy car drove up the lane. They hurried down the front steps as the auto came to a halt.

Carolyn rushed to hug Catherine. "I can't believe you are finally here."

"I'm not sure I believe it either," answered Catherine.

Then it was Elizabeth's turn while Carolyn gave Patrick a warm welcome.

"Where did you get this swell car?" asked Carolyn.

"That was my idea," said Patrick. "I needed something to perk up my spirits after those months in France. Catherine thinks it too showy, but I think it is just right."

"Do you have news of our husbands?" asked Elizabeth.

"Give them a chance to catch their breath," Carolyn ordered. "Ollie has fixed our lunch and we can have a fine chat."

As they made their way up to the porch Catherine was at Carolyn's side. "How is Mrs. Caldwell? We hesitated to come as you had written that she is failing."

"I would have been disappointed if you hadn't come. It is a matter of time, but she is comfortable."

They went into the dining room. It was the first time either Catherine or Patrick had been to the manor.

"This is a grand house," said Catherine. "I would love to see the other rooms."

"Elizabeth can take you and Patrick on a tour after we eat. I will have to check in on my patient. I don't leave her for too long a time."

They sat at the long dining table. The maids brought their lunch and poured tea.

"Now Patrick," said Elizabeth, "please tell us if you have news of our husbands. It is almost three weeks since we have heard from them."

He cleared his throat. "Well, the last time I saw them they were in good spirits, although they were tired of all the training, and the troops were getting restless. I saw them just before I sailed. Asa said they expected orders within that week. I do not know what they involved. I'm sorry I don't have better news. They did say that they will never forget the wonderful few days at the villa in Liffol Le Grand."

"Wasn't that grand? What about Celeste or Claude? Did you run into them again?" asked Elizabeth

"I saw Claude when Mrs. Du Charme came with him to the hospital. He is fitted with his new shoe, and last I heard he was hoping to join the French army."

"Why did Mrs. Du Charme go to the hospital?" asked an inquisitive Carolyn. "Did she have another sick child?"

The question caught Patrick off-guard. Should he tell Catherine in front of her friends? Another time might be wiser.

"The general's wife came to ask if our stay at her home was satisfactory."

"Did you tell her I speak French well enough that we had no problem with a language barrier?" asked Elizabeth.

"I did, and I also told her we did not lack for a thing." He smiled as he recalled. "She said she didn't want Claude fixed up well enough that he would leave her employ."

"Selfish of her," remarked Catherine.

"I'm glad that trip is behind us. What are your plans, Patrick? Are you deciding on a place to open your office?" asked Carolyn.

Patrick and Catherine looked at each other. "Do you want to tell them or shall I?"

"Dr. Hawthorne has offered to share his offices with Patrick."

Surprised looks came to the other two women.

"He has a busy practice and would like to slow down a bit. I had enough of the rush, rush, rush when I was in France. I like the slower pace of this area, and I know Catherine would embrace her old stomping grounds."

Catherine joined in, "One of the reasons we came out was for Patrick to discuss the possibility with Dr. Hawthorne."

"You mean you would give up your place in Georgetown?" asked an incredulous Elizabeth.

"We can hold onto that. If this opportunity doesn't work out, we still have that place to move back to."

"I think it is a grand idea," said Carolyn. "I know you well enough, Catherine to know you much prefer the small town to the big city."

"It is a good place to raise a family, which we hope to do."

"I'm getting used to being here, but I still miss the city," said Elizabeth. "I can't wait until this awful war is over and Andrew comes home."

"Let's not talk of war," said Carolyn. "Elizabeth you take Patrick and Catherine on a tour of the house while I go in and check on Mrs. Caldwell. Then I'll join all of you for a walk around the grounds. We can take Annie and Matthew with us. You won't believe how they've grown, Catherine."

"I have missed them. I hope they still know me."

"I'm sure they will." Carolyn left the room to tend to her patient and Elizabeth led the tour of the house.

When they were all back together, they walked toward the stables. "Father Caldwell has some fine horses. Do you have an eye for horses, Patrick?" asked Elizabeth.

"No," he replied. "I might be tempted to bet on one, but I keep my distance."

"Patrick is not fond of the odors surrounding them," chuckled Catherine.

Stuart was at the far end sitting on a mound of hay.

"That's Stuart. He used to be a jockey until he had a bad fall. It's made him sour on life and everyone in it," informed Carolyn. "I guess Mr. Caldwell took pity on him and hired him as a driver. We stay as far away from him as we can."

Luck was not with them because Stuart left the hay and came walking toward them.

"He's probably just being nosey and wants to know who you are," said Elizabeth.

Stuart had his own agenda. "You'd better keep an eye on those two," he said, pointing to Annie and Matthew. "They'll scare the horses into hurting themselves and then you'll answer to the lord and master."

"If you are referring to Mr. Caldwell, I believe you should be more respectful." Elizabeth was piqued. "I've seen you handle the horses when you think no one is looking and it isn't with kindness."

"They need to know I'm the boss."

"I don't care to continue this conversation. Mrs. Thomas and I have kept mum about your sullen attitude. If you value your position here, I suggest you change your ways." With a direct look she said, "You may step out of the way so we can show Dr. and Mrs. Burke the stables."

He swept the cap off his head and gave a lavish bow. "Whatever you say, Mrs. Caldwell."

When he was out of earshot, Patrick said, "I don't care for his look. Something isn't right with him. Perhaps it would be wise to discuss this incident with Mr. Caldwell."

Elizabeth replied, "I think he's harmless, just angry with the world."

"Elizabeth, maybe we should have a talk with Mr. Caldwell. I thought Hannah was harmless until she tried to drown me in that pond over there," said Carolyn.

Elizabeth took on a worried look. "Now you both have me concerned. I know Stuart took an instant dislike to me the first time we met. I like to take long walks and so do you Carolyn. If he went a little crazy we could be in harm's way."

"Let's not get creepy," said Carolyn.

"Nevertheless, I think we should have a good talk with Father Caldwell when he returns."

They turned and started back toward the house.

"I would feel better," advised Patrick. "There's something about the man that just doesn't click. Maybe that accident left him addled."

Carolyn sighed. "This isn't the way we would have chosen to end our lovely afternoon."

Catherine had been quiet up to that point. "It isn't, but there had to be a reason we ran into him."

Carolyn chuckled. "Could it be Providence intervening?"

"That may well be," said a sincere Catherine.

They walked their guests to the fancy car and bid them goodbye. The Burkes agreed to make one more trip out before they left for Washington.

Catherine leaned out the window and said, "We will let you know how our discussion with Dr. Hawthorne turns out."

Carolyn raised her voice above the loud hum of the engine. "We'll be waiting."

They stood holding their children's hands and waved as the fancy auto made its way down the lane.

Chapter 25

Matthew celebrated his second birthday with a three layer cake baked by Ollie. She didn't trust anyone but herself to bring it up from the kitchen and place it on the table after dinner.

He gamely blew out the two candles that decorated the top, much to the enjoyment of those in attendance. Even Will smiled and clapped.

There had been no letters from Asa or Andrew. Information in the newspapers was old news. Before the United States entered the war, amateur radio operators were allowed to publish information they received, but the government now owned the airways and it was illegal for anyone to operate radio apparatus without government consent.

William Caldwell did his best to find an amateur radio man breaking the law, but to no avail. So, at Red Gate Farm they waited.

In May, Carolyn and Elizabeth received a letter addressed to them both.

To Our Dearest Wives,

Time is short. We have returned from an engagement at St. Mihiel. Our troops performed well and I believe our allies are convinced we are able combatants.

Casualties were few. We are safe and all in one piece. We will be leaving tomorrow for another encounter.

Do not be alarmed if you don't hear from us. We will be in the thick of things. If all stays as it is, at this point, we will continue to remain together.

Patrick promised to watch over you until we return. He is a friend.

We send our love to you and ask that you give Matthew and Annie a big kiss from their homesick daddies.

Pray for us.

Your loving husbands,
Asa and Andrew

Carolyn and Elizabeth both burst into tears. How they ached to get their men back home. The letter was a relief and a worry. The men were together and safe, but would that always be the case?

**

On May 12th of 1918, Virginia Caldwell passed away. It had been many weeks since she recognized anyone or was cognizant of the world around her.

After the embalming by the Enders Funeral Service, she lay in her coffin in the parlor for three days so those who wished to pay their respects could do so.

Carolyn asked permission to move to the second floor as she was not fond of sharing the first floor with a corpse. She and Ann Catherine were given a room across from Elizabeth. It was the same room Asa had occupied when he visited the farm. There wasn't anything in the room to remind her of his presence, but she was soothed to know that he had slept in the same bed.

Elizabeth, as a member of the family, was required to be available to greet the mourners. Carolyn took care of the children. It was a busy time for Ollie in the kitchen and she kept the other help running. It seemed to keep their mind off the sadness in the big house.

Carolyn took the children away from the manor for a respite from the funeral upheaval. She walked toward the stables now that Stuart was not there. He had been relieved from his duties at Red Gate Farm. Mr. Caldwell found him a position on the other side of the county. After Elizabeth and Carolyn had talked to him about Stuart's behavior and Patrick's observation, William Caldwell was quick to get Stuart away.

Toby was working at the stables when Carolyn arrived with the two little ones. He had a big smile. "Miz' Carolyn, it sure is good to have you back here. We were all happy that you could come and nurse the Missus. It's goin' to be different around here without her. She was a nice lady."

"Toby, the house is like a tomb. I had to get out of there. I have to keep the children quiet and the best way is to get them outdoors."

Annie and Matthew were climbing on a pile of hay and laughing with delight as they threw handfuls into the air and let it fall down on them.

"The little ones don't understand. What will you do now that she's gone?" Toby asked

"I guess I will go back to Washington. I don't like living on the base. With Elizabeth here and Catherine moving back to this area, I will be alone."

"It's sorry I am to hear that. Maybe this war will be over soon and Mistah' Asa will be comin' home."

"That's my window of hope, Toby. I always keep it open."

He smiled. "Hope and prayer. You don't know how many times I'd prayed that Stuart was gone. He was a mean cuss. I'm glad Mistah' Caldwell got rid of him."

The hired man, whom Elizabeth thought was having an affair with Emily, emerged from the barn. He nodded in their direction before he went to the children and started playing with them in the hay.

"I haven't met that man," said Carolyn.

"That's Hank Phillips. Only been here three months. He's a good worker and keeps to himself pretty much."

Carolyn watched as he played with the children. He was strong and gentle in his manner. She said goodbye to Toby before she walked over to get a closer look at Emily's supposed interest. He had noble features, a full shock of sandy hair, brown eyes that lit up with his smile and a dimpled chin.

"Hello," she said. "I'm Carolyn Thomas. I've been Mrs. Caldwell's nurse."

He stopped. "Yes, ma'am. Miss Emily has told me of you and Miss Elizabeth."

"Is Miss Emily your teacher?" How cunning could she be?

"Yes, ma'am. She's teaching me so that I can get a better job. Lots of times she makes me stay longer than the others because she says I catch on faster."

"How old are you, Hank?"

"Seventeen. People always think I look older. I guess because I'm so big and strong."

"So you and Miss Emily spend a lot of time together with studies?"

"As much time as I can and still do my job on the farm. She said it makes her happy to see me eager to learn."

"I'm sure it does. Do you like Miss Emily?"

"Yes, ma'am, I do. She's a good teacher."

"She only teaches you book learning?"

He gave a questioning look. "Well, yes ma'am. What else would she be teaching me?"

Carolyn laughed. "Nothing, I guess. Thank you for playing with the children. I'm going to take them back to the house to get them cleaned up for dinner."

She shooed the children ahead of her as she walked up to the big house. Carolyn was smiling to herself. Wait until Elizabeth hears of this encounter with the hired man. So much for her suspecting Emily of carrying on an affair. He's only a seventeen-year-old farm boy who is probably just learning how to write his name. She laughed aloud.

Carolyn fed the children in the kitchen. She was pleased to not have to eat in the dining room. Once the children ate, they were bathed and settled into bed.

Upstairs, she opened her door when she heard Elizabeth come up the stairs and motioned her to come into her room.

They sat side by side on the bed. "How are you holding up?"

"Ruth should be throttled. I don't know these people and she should be here to take some of the burden off Father Caldwell. Emily and Will are doing well. I'll be glad when this is all over."

"It's good you are here. You're standing in for Andrew. I laid out the children's clothes for tomorrow."

"Thank you. That's one less worry off my mind."

"Do you want to hear something to lift your spirits?"

"I can't imagine what that would be unless you have a letter."

"Nothing that good. I met Emily's prize pupil today."

Elizabeth's interest was immediate. "What's he like?"

"Rugged, polite…seventeen."

"Seventeen!"

Millie Curtis

"Yes. It appears that Emily's only interest in him is teaching him to reach for higher goals."

"Carolyn, are you sure?"

"I'd bet on it."

"How unjust of me to read more into it. I should apologize."

"To whom? Emily doesn't know you suspected anything."

"I feel bad about even thinking it."

"If you feel that way, apologize to me and I'll forgive you. It did break the monotony of the days, didn't it?"

A smile came to Elizabeth's pretty face. "I guess it did serve some purpose. I'm going to bed so I can get through tomorrow."

"Good night, Elizabeth."

The next day was sunny with a light breeze. Carolyn stood to the side holding Ann Catherine's hand as the undertakers loaded Virginia's casket into a black horse-drawn hearse. The funeral procession consisting of friends, relatives, farmworkers and their families walked behind to a family plot that could be seen from the upper rooms of the big house. There were headstones marking the graves of Mr. Caldwell's parents, a brother and a small stone with a lamb on top marking a baby's grave. From the date marked, it could have been one of the Caldwells' children. Carolyn didn't ask.

It was a large group. Carolyn had been intent on keeping Annie by her side and hadn't been looking at the mourners assembled. When she

236

did, she looked across and found James Anderson looking at her.

Beside him stood his plump, homely Amanda. Carolyn dropped her gaze and tried to focus her attention on the minister who was presiding at the gravesite. The sight of James had taken her mind away from the funeral. She listened but did not hear the minister's words. She did hear everyone murmur, amen, and saw the men put on their hats.

The hearse rolled away and men were left to fill in the grave. Virginia's headstone was of white marble and shone brightly in the sun as though sending a ray of hope to carry on without her.

At the house, mounds of food had been prepared. Elizabeth had Matthew with her and stayed close to William Caldwell. He acted as the proud grandfather and introduced them as Andrew's wife and child.

Carolyn thought William Caldwell was holding up well. Perhaps some of his grieving had already been done. He had accepted Virginia's death and now he would have to resolve the loss.

Back at the manor, Carolyn fed Ann Catherine in the kitchen before putting her down for a nap. Annie fell asleep and Carolyn left for some fresh air. She was standing near the willows overlooking the pond when she heard, "A penny for your thoughts."

She knew the voice before turning around. "Hello, James. My thoughts aren't worth a penny."

"Thinking about the time Hannah almost did you in?"

"No, more about Asa saving my life."

"How is he?"

"I haven't had any word since their last battle."

"Will you be going back to Washington?"

"I don't know. Dr. Hawthorne said he could use an office nurse, but I have Ann Catherine."

"Find someone to take care of her."

She looked up into his handsome face. "It isn't as easy as that. I'm not sure Asa would want me to work. Besides, once he gets back, Dr. Hawthorne would have to find another to take my place. He's better off getting someone else."

"You're probably right."

"How did you know I was out here?"

"I haven't been able to keep my eyes off you."

"James don't talk like that."

"It's the truth. I've always been honest with you."

She couldn't hide her smile. "I'll grant you that. Don't you think you should be getting back before your whiny little wife comes looking for you?"

"She's making the rounds, showing off a new ring, getting the latest gossip."

"I don't care to be a target. Either you leave first or I do."

He took her hand and brought it to his lips. "I wouldn't trade these past few moments for anything, my love."

"James. Get out of here!"

He laughed and headed back toward the house.

Carolyn was upset with herself for letting him unnerve her so. She knew his sole purpose for marrying Amanda was for prestige and money and that should be enough to turn her against him. But there would always be a protected spot in her heart for James and nothing could ever pierce it.

Chapter 26

In late May, Catherine and Patrick moved back to Berryville. They were having a house built so that Patrick would be near the office. It was located on South Church Street away from Lavinia Talley's scrutiny.

There had been a big article in the *Courier* about the new doctor in town and the history of Catherine being a native of Berryville and owning the hat shop. Somehow that seemed important information so that Patrick wouldn't be looked at as an outsider.

Carolyn had moved back to the Army base and Elizabeth remained at Red Gate Farm.

Matthew was the diversion William Caldwell needed to help him through the loss of his dear wife.

May also brought news that Asa and Andrew had survived the Battle of Cantigny.

In June, Carolyn's world fell apart.

It was Ann Catherine's second birthday when she answered a knock at the door. A soldier in full dress uniform asked if he could enter.

Carolyn knew in an instant something terrible had happened.

With a trembling voice, she invited him to sit, and she took a chair opposite.

With a calm exterior he said, "The Colonel sent me. We have had news that Major Thomas was in the Battle of Belleau Wood and is missing."

The news struck Carolyn like an arrow piercing her heart.

"The Colonel sends his condolences and says if there is anything you need to call him."

After agonizing hesitation, Carolyn found her voice. "You said he is missing. You didn't say he is dead."

The soldier bearing this awful news cleared his throat. "Yes, ma'am. There were many casualties from mortar fire, grenades and tanks. At this time, we suspect but can't confirm the possibility that Major Thomas is among them."

Carolyn maintained her composure, thanked the young officer, and, once she closed the door, she fell onto the couch in a faint.

She awoke to Annie patting her face crying, "Mommy. Mommy!"

Carolyn sat up in her dazed state and pulled her precious child into her arms. She rocked her body back and forth and whispered, "Asa can't be dead, he can't."

It was a couple of hours later when she felt settled enough to call Catherine in Berryville.

Catherine listened to the dreadful account. "Oh, my good Lord, Carolyn I am so sorry. I hate this war! What are you going to do?"

"I don't know. I just can't sit here day after day waiting for them to knock on the door and tell me he's gone. I need to get news to Elizabeth. If

241

Andrew and Asa were still together maybe Andrew knows what happened."

"Carolyn, why don't you and Annie come out and stay in Elizabeth's apartment? Patrick and I can move into your old apartment in the Hawthorne House. We'll clear it with Dr. Hawthorne. Our new house will be ready in a couple of weeks."

"Do you realize that today is Annie's birthday?"

Catherine let out a compassionate sigh. "Yes. I wish I was there with you. You are a strong woman, Carolyn, but I want you to come to Berryville until this ordeal is over."

"Will you get word to Elizabeth?"

"I'll go tomorrow."

"I'm so glad I could talk with you, Catherine. I would like nothing better than to have you close at hand."

"Let me make arrangements and I will call you back before the end of the week."

"Thank you, dear friend."

When Catherine arrived at Red Gate Farm the next day, Elizabeth was helping Emily clean the classroom. Catherine walked around the big house and down the path to the old hop kiln.

The door was open. Elizabeth and Emily were laughing, talking and scrubbing away. They let out a cry of surprise when they saw Catherine come in.

Elizabeth dropped the brush she was using. "Catherine! You gave us a start."

"I came with news, but I think you should both sit down while I tell you."

The two women quickly sat.

"Carolyn telephoned me yesterday. Asa is missing."

"Oh, no," cried Elizabeth. "What happened?"

"She doesn't know and thought you may have some information from Andrew."

"I haven't heard a word. My Lord, I hope nothing has happened to Andrew."

Emily rose and put an arm around Elizabeth's shoulders. "I'm sure he's safe."

"Carolyn was doing her best to stay calm, although her voice was shaking. I told her to come and stay in your apartment over the hat shop. Patrick and I can stay at the Hawthorne House until our house is finished."

"Of course! Our dear Carolyn. What did she say?"

"I told her I would make arrangements and call her in a day or two."

"I'm sure Father Caldwell would invite her to stay here at the farm," said Emily.

Elizabeth sat as if absorbing the terrible situation. "Catherine, you said he is missing. He isn't dead?"

"I can only report what Carolyn told me. She said there were many casualties and they can't be certain Asa isn't among them."

Elizabeth put her head down on the small desk and cried.

243

Emily motioned Catherine to the door. In a soft voice she asked, "What do you think Catherine? If Asa is gone, what will she do?"

"We will handle that problem when it arises. For now the best we can do is to keep hope alive until we hear otherwise."

Elizabeth was blowing her nose when they stepped back into the room. Her eyes were swollen and her pretty face showed red blotches. "That took the wind out of my sails. I feel as limp as a rag."

"I'm sorry I had to be the one to bring the awful news, but I didn't want anyone else to bear it."

"Why don't we all go up to the house for a cup of tea?" offered Emily.

"Thank you for the invitation, but I have to be getting back to town. I left a note for Patrick and he'll be concerned if he doesn't see me and the buggy back by five."

Elizabeth hugged Catherine. "It is so good of you to make this long ride out here. If I haven't heard any bad news about Andrew, then I will presume he is safe. Where did this happen?"

"Carolyn said the soldier who talked to her called it the Battle of Belleau Wood."

"I wonder where that is?"

"I don't know and I wish I had never heard of it."

The three walked up to where the horse and buggy waited. After Catherine bid them goodbye, she climbed onto the seat, chucked the reins of the horse and headed back to Berryville.

Patrick was in the apartment when she arrived. "You didn't tell me you were going over to Red Gate. That's a long way for a woman to travel by herself. What if the buggy broke down?"

Catherine was tired. "It didn't. I left you a note."

"Still, you could have made other arrangements."

Catherine was not only tired but edgy. "And, what would they have been? I don't think you could have taken the time off from the office, and I wasn't going to tell anyone else."

"I was concerned."

"Worry about your patients and not about me, Patrick. I'm a big girl." She threw her sweater over a chair. "I'm going to heat up stew for supper."

He looked at her with a discerning eye. "Being upset with me isn't going to bring Asa back, Catherine."

She turned and looked at him before she went into his open arms. "I'm sorry, Patrick. You're right. I can't help thinking about poor Carolyn."

"It'll work out. I cleared our move into the Hawthorne House with Thaddeus. Call Carolyn and tell her this apartment will be ready for her by Monday. That's the best we can do for her now."

Her face fell against his shoulder before she looked up and kissed his cheek. "I'll call her in the morning. Does left-over stew for supper sound all right?"

"Anything. I'm famished."

245

Chapter 27

When Carolyn locked the door to the house on the Army base, it was like closing a chapter in her life. It had been a week since the soldier came with the news of Asa missing.

Her fears were that she may never know the truth. She held onto the possibility that Andrew may have seen what happened. Surely word would come from him before long. Even if it was the tragic news that Asa was killed, which she didn't allow herself to dwell on, it would be confirmation, and she would have to get on with her life. Not knowing was hell on earth.

A week later she settled into the apartment over the hat shop, thankful that Lavinia didn't rush across the street the minute she arrived.

Her sense of adventure had dissolved and in its place was a hollow, gut-wrenching feeling of loss. She and Asa had talked about future plans, but what future was there for her now?

Catherine and Patrick both arrived that evening. Their warm embraces gave her solace.

Ann Catherine had not been put to bed for the night and she seemed as glad to see them as did Carolyn.

Patrick read her a bedtime story as Catherine and Carolyn went to the kitchen to talk.

"How is Annie?" asked Catherine. "She doesn't flash her ready smile."

"I have tried to keep the gravity of the situation to myself. Keep a stiff upper lip, pull yourself up by the bootstraps, keep life going as she knows it and all that other folderol, but not knowing haunts my very being. She's a perceptive child and knows something is wrong."

Patrick came into the kitchen and pulled out a chair to sit at the table with them. "Flopsy, Mopsy, Cottontail and Peter are all done for the night. She's fast asleep."

Carolyn smiled. "Thank you, Patrick. When was the last time you saw Asa?"

"Andrew, Asa and I went to a café before they left for their first engagement. It was shortly before I left. They were pleased that I was coming back and, once again, asked that I watch over you and Elizabeth. Both were in good spirits."

A faint smile appeared on Carolyn's face. "I was so happy they were together. They are as close as brothers."

"Carolyn, Catherine and I have been talking. Not knowing for sure the condition of your husband has to be in your mind day and night. I've discussed this with Thaddeus and we would like to have you consider taking a position as office nurse. We are very busy and could use your help and…"

"I could take care of Annie," interrupted Catherine. "It would keep us both busy. This would only be until Asa returns."

"And, if he doesn't return?"

Catherine laid a gentle hand on Carolyn's arm. "You make decisions as they arise."

Carolyn faltered. "I…I don't know."

"Ann Catherine is an easy child to care for and she is my godchild. Carolyn, you need to keep your mind occupied."

She sat silent for a minute. "I won't say that I wouldn't like to get back to nursing because there is nothing I would like better."

"Then say, yes," encouraged Patrick. "The arrangement will keep both you ladies busy. You can start when you're ready. Dr. Hawthorne will be happy to hear you will be returning."

"I want to get out to see Elizabeth."

Catherine was eager. "I'll go with you if you'd like company. We can take the horse and buggy."

Sitting and talking with her friends had brightened Carolyn's disposition. "Let's make a day of it. I'll pack a picnic and we can sit by the old mill for lunch."

"Agreed," said Catherine. "When do you want to go?"

"Give me a couple of days. We can go out on Thursday."

"I'll pray there's no rain," kidded Catherine.

"Then it's all settled?" asked Patrick.

"It's settled," answered Carolyn. "You can tell Dr. Hawthorne I will be at the office at eight o'clock sharp next Monday."

After Patrick and Catherine left, Carolyn sat and thought over what she had just agreed to. She was sure Asa wouldn't mind her taking the position as long as Annie was well-cared for. After all, he wasn't there to give his permission. Perhaps this was Catherine's Providence at work.

Two days later, Catherine pulled the buggy in front of the hat shop on Main Street.

Carolyn and Annie were ready and waiting in the foyer. Carolyn no sooner turned the key in the lock when she heard, "Yoo-hoo."

She knew who it was before she turned and let out a mild oath.

"Good morning, Mrs. Talley," called Catherine. "You've caught us just as we are about to leave."

"My goodness it seems you young ladies are always on the go. Catherine, I just wanted to say how pleased we are that Dr. Burke has decided to settle here and you are back home."

Catherine was truthful. "It is good to be home."

"Are you going to open the hat shop?"

"That belongs to Mrs. Caldwell. I will be kept busy with the new house."

"Yes, I would love to see it. I understand you and Dr. Burke are staying at the Hawthorne House until it is ready?"

Did nothing escape Lavinia?

"Yes."

"I thought it odd that you would move from this apartment. Is there a reason Carolyn has come back?"

Carolyn had put the picnic basket in the rear of the buggy and placed her daughter next to Catherine on the seat. She was climbing in. "Good morning, Mrs. Talley. I can speak for myself. I needed a rest and what better place to rest than here in the lethargy of Berryville? We have to hurry, Catherine."

"We'll talk again, Mrs. Talley," said Catherine to the round, little woman with mouth agape. She tapped the reins and the buggy pulled away.

"That windbag! At least the word isn't out about Asa," said a relieved Carolyn. "I think I would have crowned her if she pried into what happened."

"Leave her behind. Don't let her dampen our day. We are going to have a picnic and see Elizabeth. What could be more uplifting?"

In Millwood, they went to the very same spot Carolyn had gone to with James Anderson on the first day she met him. They had been on their way to Red Gate Farm for her to care for Virginia Caldwell.

The stone grist mill looked majestic. A fine mist rose from the spillway, much to Annie's delight. Carolyn smiled to herself as she looked around and recalled how she had been so nervous that she couldn't eat a bite. That was four years ago.

"Let's move the blanket over. I feel damp-ness from this spot," said Catherine. "Come on, Annie. You help me carry the blanket and your mommy will bring the basket."

Carolyn followed as if in a trance.

"Are you all right?"

She snapped to. "Yes, letting memories carry me away."

"Pleasant ones, I hope," said Catherine as she spread the blanket on the grass.

"I think so. I brought ham sandwiches, boiled eggs and cookies. There's tea in the jug."

They sat on the blanket while Carolyn doled out the napkins and food. Catherine poured each a mug of tea.

"What is Annie going to drink?" she asked.

"She can sip my tea. I thought milk might spoil, and I didn't have another jug for water. Catherine, we didn't get word to Elizabeth that we were coming. What if she isn't there?"

"Where else would she be? Certainly not visiting her parents."

Carolyn laughed. "That's for sure. I'm glad she got out from under her mother's ruling thumb. Her father's a good egg."

"He is. Don't you wonder what brought them together?"

"I don't know. People change. I can't picture them as young lovebirds."

"Or old ones." Catherine chuckled at the thought. "Let's eat. I'm looking forward to seeing Elizabeth and Matthew."

251

At the large farm, they found Elizabeth pushing Matthew in a long swing hung from the strong limb of an oak tree. When she saw the buggy, she stopped the swing, almost spilling Matthew to the ground.

Tears ran down her face as she raced to meet them.

"Elizabeth what is wrong?" cried Catherine.

Emily hurried from the house.

Elizabeth was crying and couldn't get any words out.

"It's Andrew," informed Emily as she hurried up. "Word came yesterday that he has been wounded."

"Dear God!" exclaimed Carolyn.

Elizabeth was drying tears with an apron she wore.

"Come inside," said Emily. "We were going to get news to you Catherine, and Carolyn, we weren't aware that you were here. But, I'm very glad you are. Andrew has sent a letter. Doris can come and watch the children while we go inside and read it."

Elizabeth had composed herself. "I'm sorry. It is just so good to see both of you. Carolyn have you heard from Asa?"

A lump jumped into her throat and all she could do was shake her head.

Catherine put her arms around both of her friends. "Emily has the right idea. Let's go in and read what Andrew has to say."

Ollie brought them refreshments as they sat in the parlor. Emily was asked to read the letter because Elizabeth knew she couldn't get through it without breaking down.

Dearest Elizabeth,

I am not sure how to start this letter. I know it has been too long since you have had any word from me, but it was not my choice.

We have been heavily engaged in different battles since April. This last one was at a place called Belleau Wood. It was a fierce encounter where we lost many of our men.

I regret to say that I was hit by shrapnel and am lying on an uncomfortable iron bed in the naval hospital in Brest. Don't be alarmed. I was hit in the legs, knocking me into a fox hole, which may have saved my life.

Smoke from the booming guns, tanks and grenades made it almost impossible to know who were our men and who were the enemy.

I lay in that hole in the ground until the roar of battle was over, until our medical corps came searching.

I have had three surgeries. Although I feel pain and numbness, the doctors assure me I will walk again. I fear my military career is over.

I pray that Carolyn has had word from Asa. My last glimpse of him was when he was rallying his men. Then there was a big explosion. I saw a couple of mules go down, and then I was hit.

I thought he may have been wounded, but there is no record of him here. When I am up on my feet, I will see to his whereabouts.

The war and battles go on. This is June and I can only wonder how much longer. Depending on my ability, once I am released, I will either be sent home or kept on to do paperwork.

I miss you and Matthew so much. My mind keeps bringing up memories of happy times we've had together. I smile when I think of how standoffish you were in the beginning. But, being truthful with myself, I probably came across a little too cocky. After all, I had never had a girl turn me down. In a sense, you clipped my wings.

I trust all is going well at Red Gate. They have held all the letters you have written. I was informed they will arrive this afternoon by a volunteer with the Red Cross. Those letters will catch me up on the news.

Give Matthew a big hug and kiss for me.

My love knows no bounds for both of you.

Your devoted husband,

Andrew

The women sat in silence as Emily folded the letter and placed it back in the envelope.

Catherine broke the quiet of the room. "We didn't want to hear that Andrew has been wounded Elizabeth. At least you know that he is safe. It sounds as though he will be coming home with some scars, but he will be coming and all in one piece."

She turned to Carolyn. "I know it didn't answer your question about Asa. Maybe there are more answers across the sea than there are in Washington. Keep that window of hope alive, Carolyn."

"It is of some comfort to know that Andrew had seen him, and I know he will leave no stone unturned in his search for what happened."

To change the atmosphere in the room, Catherine informed, "The good news is that Carolyn will be the office nurse for Patrick and Dr. Hawthorne. I will be caring for Ann Catherine, while she is working."

"That is good to hear," said Emily. "You shouldn't waste your nursing talents by sitting around with your mind conjuring up all kinds of dreadful possibilities."

"I get lots of advice," said Carolyn. "I am looking forward to doing some nursing. You're right, Emily, I will be better off than watching the idle hours pass away."

"Goodness, you helped me out of my miseries. I could never have crawled out of the bottle by myself."

"Well, this is enough reminiscing," joined in Elizabeth. "Let's go out and relieve Doris so she can resume her duties in the house. Do you have to get back to town or would you like to see the gardens Emily and I have started?"

"I wasn't aware you liked to garden," said Catherine.

"Neither was I, until Emily asked me to help her plant some seeds. We've got vegetables and flowers coming up."

"I thought you preferred to look perfect and have maids do all your work," chided Carolyn.

"That's the old Elizabeth. I've found a new one since I've been here at the farm."

"Does Mr. Caldwell approve? What I mean is, doesn't tending a garden look like hired hands work?"

"We dress for dinner, promptly at six, and everyone is happy."

Carolyn laughed. "Yes, dinner at six. How I hated to sit in that dining room."

Emily gave her opinion. "With Ruth not here, everyone seems more relaxed. Will is doing a good job of overseeing the workings of the farm, and Father Caldwell is captivated by Matthew. I sometimes think it was Mother Caldwell who was too stiff and unbending with propriety."

"Emily!" Elizabeth exclaimed

"We'll keep it to ourselves," she said. "Let's go out and tour these gardens before our good friends have to be off."

Chapter 28

As June turned into July and July turned into August, there was no further word about Asa. Carolyn had not yet succumbed to the possibility that he wouldn't be coming home.

During the week, she created a routine that didn't falter from day to day: up at six-thirty, feed and dress Annie, don her nurse's uniform, lock the apartment door at seven-thirty and walk the three blocks to Catherine and Patrick's new home before arriving at the Hawthorne House at seven-fifty.

On Saturdays, she was kept busy with house work that couldn't be done during the week.

Sunday started the day by attending services at Grace Episcopal Church, where she sat with Catherine and Patrick, then hurried back to the apartment to avoid Lavinia Talley's ongoing questions.

The town gossips conjured up ideas as to why Carolyn had returned to Berryville. It was known that Asa was missing in the war. That fact became fodder for those who gobbled up rumors. They ranged from him being a prisoner of war, to being a deserter, to being run over by a German tank, and the most outrageous of all that he had left Carolyn for a French woman.

Andrew had written that he would be coming home. He had no news of Asa, although he was still checking every possible lead.

Carolyn thought how fortunate for Elizabeth that she would be reunited with her husband. Perhaps Andrew would walk with a cane and carry some battle scars, but, he was alive.

She had made a trip out to Gaylord to visit her family only once since she had returned to Berryville. It was good to see them, but she was a different Carolyn than the girl who had grown up in that tenant house.

Her brothers would stop by, when they came to town, with gifts of food from her mother. Her parents rarely ventured away from home so Carolyn would send letters.

One morning, Carolyn was in the back yard hanging laundered clothes on the line when there was a knock at the back gate. Ann Catherine was playing with her dolls in the gazebo.

Before Carolyn lifted the latch, she asked, "Who is it?"

A quiet malevoice answered, "James."

She was caught by surprise. "James Anderson?"

"What other James do you know who would discreetly come to your back gate?"

She hurried to lift the latch. It was a struggle so between them both, the gate opened enough to allow him to enter.

"I haven't opened that gate all summer."

"That's obvious. Look how it tore up the grass." He smiled and any misgivings she may have had about letting him in dissipated on the spot.

He was nattily dressed in a pin stripe summer suit. He took off the boater hat he wore over his wavy black hair. As tall and handsome as ever, it was all Carolyn could do to keep her calm demeanor.

"What are you doing here, and why did you come in the back?"

"I have wanted to come for weeks to tell you how truly sorry I am to hear of Asa's misfortune."

"Which rumor have you heard?"

"I went over to Red Gate Farm and talked with Andrew's wife. I knew she would have the true story. As far as coming to the back gate, it was because I didn't want Lavinia Talley to see me."

"You were lucky I was out here."

"If you hadn't been, I would have come to the front door."

"What if someone else saw you come down the lane?"

"They didn't. I made sure of that."

Carolyn shook her head. "I don't know how you can be sure, but now that you're here and have torn up the lawn, come over and sit in the gazebo. Annie's playing with her dolls."

When they entered, Ann Catherine looked up and ran to her mother. She didn't say a word.

"She's shy. Except for Catherine and Patrick, she sticks close to me."

She wiped off benches with a dish towel she'd slung over her shoulder and James took a seat. She pulled Annie onto her lap and sat opposite.

"Carolyn, I came to see for myself how you are doing."

A wan smile appeared on her comely face. "I'm managing. Not knowing if Asa is alive or dead takes its toll. I try not to dwell on it. The longer there is no news, the less I hold out hope. Hope is all I have, James." She swallowed hard to quell the tears she felt welling up.

He pretended to not see her discomfort and sat relaxed with one leg crossed over the other. "I can only imagine how difficult it is for you. Do you need anything?"

She shook her head.

"You know there is nothing I wouldn't do for you." He uncrossed his legs and leaned forward. "Carolyn, what are you going to do if he doesn't make it back?"

"Why are you asking?"

"We were very close friends at one time. I am concerned about your welfare. Now you have a child to care for also. I have plenty of money and can take care of both of you."

Carolyn was skeptical. She looked directly into is eyes. "James, I cared deeply for you. When you decided to marry Amanda, I was devastated, but it opened my eyes. I don't know for certain what you're proposing, but I believe I can make a good guess. No James, if I find that I will be alone then I will meet the challenge. For now, I have the position working for Patrick and Dr. Hawthorne. I don't see that changing. I can make it on my own."

A wry smile appeared before he rose to leave. "You are a stubborn woman."

She answered with confidence, "At times it has helped me from making a bad decision."

She put Annie down off her lap to resume her play with her dolls as she followed James into the yard.

"I am happy you came by. Don't worry about me, James. I know that whatever happens, I will be fine."

When they reached the gate, he kissed her forehead. "Always we part as friends. I wish it were more."

"Three years ago, so did I. We part as we should. You'll never change. Money and power. If not Amanda there will some other well-heeled lass coming along."

He touched the tip of her nose with his finger. "You know me well. Goodbye, Carolyn."

"Goodbye, James."

Carolyn walked back to where Annie was playing. She picked her up and held her close, "Oh, my sweet little girl. What is to become of us?"

Chapter 29

The last week in August William Caldwell hosted a welcome home party for Andrew. Carolyn and Ann Catherine rode over to Red Gate Farm with Catherine and Patrick. The snappy little car was crowded, but they were so enthused about seeing Andrew they didn't care.

The day was hot. Tables of food had been set up under the large oak trees, where the temperature was a few degrees cooler.

Elizabeth came hurrying to meet them when she saw them coming. "I am so happy to see all of you. Andrew is sitting up on the knoll. It's the coolest place on the lawn. I had to convince him not to wear that hot Army uniform.

The few neighbors we invited have come and gone. There is plenty of food, water, lemonade, tea, and Father Caldwell had them ice down some beer. First, you must come and say hello to Andrew. He has lost weight and is pale. We thought it would be good for him to be among friends, perhaps bring him out of the doldrums."

They followed Elizabeth to where Andrew sat in his mother's wheelchair.

Carolyn could not restrain herself. She handed Annie to Catherine and ran to throw her arms around him.

"Carolyn, I did my best. You have lost your husband, and I have lost my best friend."

This once strong, noble, handsome man was close to tears.

She kissed his cheek and smoothed his auburn hair. "I know you did, but you must mend first before you continue your search. We are all grateful that you are home."

His usual sparkly green eyes were lifeless.

"Andrew, Catherine and Patrick are here with me. We rode in Patrick's new car. It's a nifty little thing. You'll have to go for a ride with him before we leave."

A slight smile creased his lips when Catherine and Patrick came up.

"Andrew," said Patrick as he clasped his hand. "Resting in your mother's wheelchair, I see."

"Being lazy," answered Andrew. "I'm supposed to be up and walking as much as possible, but I don't seem to have much stamina. I do quite a good job at hobbling."

Catherine sat Annie down and she ran to her mother.

Andrew watched her. "She's a lovely little one, Carolyn. Her father would be proud of her. I used to kid Asa about how it was good she looked more like her mother than her father."

There was no humor in Andrew's tone.

"I'm sure you were surprised at how Matthew has grown since you saw him last December."

"It's taking time for him to get used to me. I think his grandfather has taken my place."

It was so unlike him to be downhearted and feeling sorry for himself. The war had left its mark both mentally and physically.

Catherine stepped forward and took Andrew's hand. "I'm glad to see you. We are all in the process of healing. The cares of today will pass with time."

"I'm sorry I'm not better company."

Elizabeth came to his side. "I think it's time we all get a plate of food. You have to be hot and tired after driving over those rough roads."

Carolyn laughed. "We were packed in that little car like sardines in a tin can. Annie had the only comfortable seat because she was on my lap."

"Andrew, what do you say to us hobbling over to get a cold beer?" asked Patrick.

"I think you are trying to get me out of this chair."

"That could be part of it. Who wheels that ungainly thing around? I trust Elizabeth doesn't push it."

"There's plenty of help around who feel sorry for me."

"Not any sorrier than you feel for yourself."

Andrew shrugged a shoulder.

"Come on. Grab that cane. I'm thirsty. I haven't had a cold beer since I left France."

Doris came by with Matthew in hand. "Miz' Carolyn, I can take Annie with me. We're going back to the big swing."

Annie went without a fuss when she saw Matthew, allowing Carolyn time to chat with her friends.

Andrew pulled himself up from the chair and took the cane hanging on the back. The women went on ahead while Patrick slowed to Andrew's pace.

The five of them sat at a round wood table to enjoy their repast. They talked about the days in France at Christmastime when they had all been together.

"Whose idea was that anyway?" asked Patrick.

"It was Catherine's," Carolyn answered.

"I wouldn't have thought of it, if it hadn't been for you and Elizabeth coming up with the half-brained idea of joining the Nurse Corps and the Hello Girls."

"Oh, you would too. You were worrying about the French women seducing the American men."

Andrew smiled at Patrick. "You did tell her about the French general's wife, didn't you?"

"You mean the one who owned that grand villa we stayed in?" asked Catherine.

Patrick wrinkled his forehead. "I haven't found the right time."

"Well, pray tell. When will you? You've been home since April." Catherine was to the point.

"Do tell us," said Elizabeth. "I want to hear it."

"The general's wife is a rather charming and alluring woman. She invited me up to the villa for food and music on New Year's Eve."

"Tell me you didn't go," said Catherine.

"I thought about it."

"And?"

"And, I went. The food was delicious, the music enjoyable. She invited me to spend the night."

"My goodness," said Elizabeth. "I don't believe it."

"I do," said Carolyn. "She didn't let us stay in that stately home without expecting some kind of payment."

"Continue, Patrick. I'm all ears,' said Catherine.

"We all are," said the others.

"Maybe I shouldn't have brought it up," Andrew apologized.

"No, it's good you did. What happened was that I turned her down. Not that I didn't consider it, but I thought of you, dear Catherine. I put on my coat, said goodbye and walked back to Brest."

"Walked back?" asked Catherine.

"The moon was full and the night was cold. Just what I needed to quell the heat that woman had stirred. Last I heard, she was turning her charms on someone else."

"I'll bet he stayed the night," said Carolyn.

Patrick laughed. "I'm sure it wasn't the first time. I'm relieved we've all heard this sad tale." He turned to Catherine. "Shall I tell them the good news or do you want to?"

"After hearing that story, the good news is that you didn't take up the floozy's offer," said a bothered Catherine.

Patrick offered a coy smile. "I wouldn't call her a floozy."

"I would," came Catherine's reply. She changed to a more pleasant tone, "The absolute good news is that we will be filling one of the bedrooms in our new home with a baby."

Carolyn jumped up from her chair. "Catherine, how wonderful for you both." She ran to her good friend and hugged her.

Elizabeth followed. "How is this one going?"

"Wonderful. Entirely different from my first misfortune. We may have a Christmas baby."

"How could you keep that a secret?" asked Carolyn.

"After the last disaster you two helped me through, I wanted to be sure about this one. Besides," she patted Patrick's arm. "I now have two good doctors looking after me."

Andrew perked up. "That is good news. I've heard that a baby is God's sign that the world should go on."

Patrick finished the last sip of beer in the bottle he held. He took out his pocket watch. "Almost time for us to be heading back," he announced. "But, not before I take Andrew for a spin in what Catherine calls my gaudy car."

"I'm up for it, if it'll hold a cripple."

Patrick did not offer sympathy. "Drag your crippled body down there, and we'll see if the car complains."

Andrew grabbed his cane and slowly made his way to the car where Patrick waited.

"It's good to see Andrew among friends. I feel so bad that I can't do more to brighten his mood. He grieves for Asa and blames himself for his failure at not finding any trace. How are you doing, Carolyn?"

"I keep holding onto a thread of hope, but as the days pass it gets thinner and thinner. It has been four months. Once a year has passed and I have no final proof, I will resolve myself to the fact that he isn't coming home. Only then will I make decisions about my future."

"You are brave, Carolyn. I think I would fall apart if I were in your situation."

"You're strong, too, Elizabeth. You would handle it as I do."

When Patrick brought Andrew back, he drove up onto the lawn and stopped the car next to the table where the women were seated. He hopped out and let Andrew get out by himself.

"Patrick, you shouldn't have driven on the lawn," admonished his wife.

"I had Andrew's permission. It will save everyone a few steps."

Andrew came to where they sat. "Elizabeth, we need to think about a jazzy little car like that. Beats riding a horse."

"You'll be back on a horse," said Patrick. "Come in next week and I'll take a look at what kind of a job the Army surgeons did."

"I'll be there. Before you go, I want to tell all of you how good it is to see you. I know I have a ways to go before I feel like my old self. But, you have brought me the first light moments I've had in six months. God bless you."

They said their goodbyes before Patrick, Catherine, Carolyn and Annie jammed into the little auto for the bumpy ride back to Berryville.

It was strengthening for them to all be together. There was a void without Asa, and Carolyn wondered if the hurt would ever go away.

Chapter 30

The next week Andrew appeared in Patrick's office. Elizabeth had ridden into town with him because she wanted to check on the hat shop and look over the dresses in Irene Butler's shop.

While she was in the hat shop, Mr. Miller from the bank knocked on the door. "How fortuitous that you've come by, Mrs. Caldwell. I had a gentleman in the other day who is interested in buying the place."

"Do you mean the shop and the apartment?"

"Yes."

"I will have to think about it."

"He's willing to meet the asking price. I just have to draw the papers together."

"Mrs. Thomas and her daughter are living up there. I wouldn't want to place another burden on her if she had to move."

"I understand. You do realize this is the first real offer we've had since you left over a year ago."

"Of course, I realize that. No one wants to sell the place more than I do. Mrs. Thomas is my friend and I will have to talk with her first."

"It isn't wise to let this one slip by."

"I will have an answer for you later today."

"I'll be at the bank all day," he said and left.

Elizabeth sat in a chair to decide how she should approach Carolyn. Heaven knows Carolyn had enough to worry about regarding Asa. Red Gate Farm was too far away to offer that she could stay there. Perhaps Carolyn could stay with Catherine and help her when the baby comes. Then Elizabeth became concerned that Catherine could no longer take care of Ann Catherine and what would Carolyn do then. The more she thought the more muddled her mind became. She left the chair, picked up her pocketbook, locked the door and headed to Irene Butler's dress shop.

She didn't find any dress that appealed to her. With an apology to Irene, she left to meet her husband at the Hawthorne house.

Andrew and Elizabeth planned to eat at the Battletown Inn for lunch. They asked Carolyn to join them.

"I can be there a few minutes after twelve. You can order me some green fried tomatoes and a glass of tea. That way it will be ready when I get there, and I won't be late getting back here to the office."

Andrew, slowed by using the cane, and Elizabeth went on ahead. People on the street smiled or tipped their hats as they went by. The whole town was aware of Andrew's injury. Elizabeth was thankful for the few extra minutes so she could tell Andrew about the buyer for the hat shop.

He shook his head. "I'm not sure. I know it would take a load off your shoulders. Certainly there's room at Red Gate, but Carolyn seems content here in town. Let's pose the situation to her when she comes for lunch. She wouldn't forgive us if we weren't truthful with her."

Elizabeth touched his hand as they sat at a small table. "I know we should."

"Do you want to know what Patrick said about my examination?"

"Certainly. I should have asked that first."

"He said the Army doctors did a good job. He also ordered me to get busy around the farm to build up the muscle I've lost."

"Busy doing what?"

"Pitching hay, walking the horses, mucking out the stables, carrying water. You know, all that stuff we hire others to do."

Elizabeth laughed. "And, what did you say to that?"

"I knew he nudged me in the right direction. I have been feeling sorry for myself and allowing others to pity me. When I think of the maimed men I saw and the ones who gave their lives, I know how much better off I am. I apologize for not being the man you married, but I promise to do my best to regain my former self."

"We've all changed, Andrew. I love you no matter what."

He squeezed her hand with gentle pressure.

When Carolyn arrived, the waiter was quick to bring their food.

Midway into the meal Elizabeth told Carolyn about the prospective buyer.

Carolyn accepted the news and replied. "It's about time. You've wanted to get rid of that place for a year."

"You and Ann Catherine are always welcome at the farm," advised Andrew.

"That's kind of you. I'm fine with my situation as it is. Do you think the buyer would rent the apartment?"

"I didn't think to ask. He's a bachelor accountant. I can ask Mr. Miller when I talk with him this afternoon. How long will Catherine be able to care for Annie?"

"I was concerned so I asked her. She says Patrick has insisted that she have a woman to care for the house and that includes Ann Catherine."

"How did she accept that suggestion?"

Carolyn gulped some tea before she laughed. "You know Catherine. She likes to do things herself. She told him she wouldn't consent to anyone except Mattie."

That brought a smile from Andrew and raised eyelids from Elizabeth. "Oh, my. What did he say to that?" she asked.

"Patrick met her challenge. He told her he was going to get in touch with Mattie and ask if she and Jacob would consider coming out here."

"Where would they stay?"

Patrick will have a small house built for them behind his and Catherine's. Jacob can take care of the yard. Same set-up as in Georgetown."

"What if they don't want to come?"

"Mattie will make the decision, and I don't see her wanting anyone else helping Catherine with a new baby. She loves Ann Catherine, too. If Mattie comes, she will be a life saver for me."

"That doesn't solve your problem of a place to live if I sell the hat shop."

"I'm not worried. Until you talk with Mr. Miller and sign papers, I'm settled for now. I can only meet one problem at a time."

Andrew spoke up. "Carolyn, I have the names of the men still alive who served under Asa. I am going to write to each one to see if they can enlighten us as to what happened that day he was declared missing."

"Don't you think the Army has already done that?"

"In time of war many routines get twisted. I will do my own investigation."

Carolyn glanced up at the clock on the wall. "Goodness, I don't even have time for dessert. Thank you for lunch. It was a pleasure. I usually wrap a peanut butter sandwich and eat in my old apartment at the Hawthorne House."

Elizabeth came alive. "Carolyn, do you think Dr. Hawthorne would let you and Annie stay there?"

"You tell me what Mr. Miller has up his sleeve and I'll go on from that point." She hugged both Elizabeth and Andrew and hurried back to work.

**

When the first of October rolled around, so did Mattie and Jacob. Patrick paid for their fare both on the train and for the ride from the Bluemont station to Berryville. He had given Herbert Marks a generous tip and told him to treat them with respect.

Patrick met the couple when they arrived in town. He took the horse and buggy that Catherine preferred to the automobile. It was good he did because, with Mattie and the two big boxes they'd packed, the combined bulk would never fit into Patrick's little car.

He drove them the three blocks to the house, where Catherine came out to meet them.

"Mattie, I can't tell you how glad I am to see you and Jacob. We'll go on to the little house so you can put your belongings inside."

The small house had gone up quickly with Mr. Ritter's crew working from dawn to dusk. With a front porch and curlicues of decorative wood, it looked like a gingerbread cottage with two bedrooms, one bathroom, a large living room and u-shaped kitchen.

It only took one look at Mattie's face to see how pleased she was.

"Do you think you'll be comfortable here?" asked Catherine.

"It'll do," replied Mattie.

Luck was on Carolyn's side because the accountant who bought Elizabeth's hat shop did not want to close the deal until after the first of the year. Something about it being more beneficial to him regarding taxes. The waiting period to sign the papers gave Carolyn time to look for a place to live.

Andrew's inquiries had not been fruitful. He received letters from relatives of some of the men who were unable to respond themselves. He saw men's names on the list of missing that he knew were dead. They had been blown to bits before his eyes. He worked diligently to right the wrongs.

The Army had given him the choice of staying in the service or being discharged. He would be relegated to a desk doing paperwork, which wasn't to his liking. His strength was returning, and although he would always walk with a limp, he was back to riding horses. He and Elizabeth were happy to remain at Red Gate Farm.

Christmas did not signal a new birth at the Burke house. Catherine produced an eight pound baby boy two weeks before, Joseph Patrick.

Mattie and Jacob decided to stay longer. "Miz' Catherine. You needs to have help 'til this little one be's on his feet."

Catherine didn't protest.

William Caldwell invited everyone to Red Gate Farm on Christmas Eve. It had been a year since the three daring young women made the voyage to see their husbands. One long year since Carolyn had seen her beloved Asa. The war had been declared over on the eleventh day of the eleventh month on the eleventh hour. She feared she had lost all hope. The hope she had clung to for so long.

Patrick paid Herbert Marks a handsome sum to take them to and from Red Gate Farm. No trains were due at the Bluemont station.

The evening was cool but invigorating. Candles were lit in every window when they reached the farm. Inside was a large decorated tree with gaily wrapped presents under it.

Even on Christmas Eve, dinner was promptly at six o'clock. During the middle of dinner and lively conversation, Doris announced a visitor had arrived who asked to see Miz' Carolyn."

Carolyn's heart stopped. The only person that popped into her mind was James Anderson. It would not bother him one bit to come to Red Gate as one of the family and ask to see her privately.

With an embarrassed clearing of her throat, she said, "Please excuse me."

With her mind set to give James a piece of it, she went into the foyer.

"Hello, Carolyn."

She screamed. "Asa! Oh my good Lord, Asa!" She ran into his arms and almost swooned.

The others had heard her cry and came hurrying from the dining room.

"Asa!" shouted Andrew and broke down in tears.

Elizabeth and Catherine stood crying, while Patrick and William Caldwell tried to keep a stiff upper lip. Tears of joy and relief, hugs, pats on the back, it was a wonderful reunion.

William Caldwell stepped forward. "Come in, dear boy, and tell us all about it."

Asa held onto Carolyn as to never let her go.

The group started back to the dining room with Carolyn and Asa at the rear.

She whispered, "How did you know I was here?"

"You had written that you were caring for Mrs. Caldwell. I took a gamble you and your friends would all be together at Christmas. If I was wrong, I knew Mr. Caldwell could get me into Washington tomorrow to spend Christmas Day with the two people I love most in this world." He kissed her hand.

The happy group took their seats around the familiar dining table.

"Doris, set a place for our guest before you go down to the kitchen and have Ollie prepare a healthy plate of warm food for Major Thomas," ordered William Caldwell.

He explained, "Will and Emily have gone to visit her relatives over the holidays. They will be delighted to learn you are home safe."

"Where are the children?" asked Asa.

"Asleep upstairs. One of the hired help is watching them," answered Carolyn. She took his hand in hers, under the table, protected from view of the others.

Doris appeared with a heaping plate of roast turkey, potatoes, cranberry dressing, gravy and turnips.

"Go right ahead. We were just into the dessert portion," said William.

"I am famished." Asa was truthful.

Andrew was brighter than he had been since he returned home. "We are all on edge waiting to hear your tale."

"It didn't escape me that you are using a cane, so I believe you have a tale of your own to tell," was Asa's reply.

"I want you to know that I did my best to find you. We feared the worst, as you probably suspect."

"I have an old French couple to thank for finding me. Just before dark set in, villagers came scavenging for anything they could use. I was knocked unconscious and laying under debris. When they rolled me over to take my pocket watch, I moaned." He laughed. "That probably scared them out of their shoes. Somehow, they got me to my feet, and I laid in their wagon as they took me to their little place."

"This was at Belleau Wood," said Patrick, more as a statement than a question.

Asa nodded as he put another forkful of potatoes into his mouth.

Patrick looked at Andrew, "The same place you were wounded."

"I lost track of you, Asa. Last I saw you were leading a bayonet charge. There was a big explosion and two mules went down. Thick smoke and dust were everywhere and then I got hit and ended up in a foxhole."

Asa paused. "It will not be disabling?"

Andrew smiled. "Patrick assures me that, if I keep to his orders, the most I will end up with is a limp. I can still show off my battle scars." His good nature had returned.

"Good to hear," answered Asa. "It took me a month to recover my wits. Twice I tried to get back to the troops but had to turn back because the area was alive with Germans. Once the armistice was announced I began again trying to find a way back. The headquarters had been dismantled and troop ships had sailed, so I bargained with a cargo captain to let me work my way back to the States." He interrupted himself, "May I have a piece of that apple pie?"

The others roared with laughter.

Asa continued between bites. "We got to New York and I had earned enough money on the ship to send a telegram to the War Department. I told them I was alive and would they send money by Western Union so I could buy a ticket to Washington. They thought it was a hoax and wouldn't forward any.

I was penniless, so I bummed my way to Baltimore and then bummed my way to Berryville. Believe me, it was a slow process. People were good about giving me a lift. I rode in wagons, trucks and even had a ride on a motorcycle.

When I finally reached Berryville, I borrowed a horse from the stable and told Mr. Hardesty that William Caldwell would pay for it. He said as long as I knew William and Andrew, he was sure he would get paid.

So here I am, dressed like a peasant, looking like a bum and tired to the core."

Carolyn kissed his rough, bearded face. "Asa, you look wonderful to me!"

He slipped his arm around her waist.

Andrew Caldwell, with a wide smile on his face and his green eyes glistening, stood with glass in hand. "This calls for a toast; to our good friend, Asa Thomas, whom we feared was lost. Welcome home!"

"May I add," said an exuberant Carolyn. "To put this in Catherine's words, I believe we are all witnesses to the hand of Providence at work."

"Amen!"

COMMENTS FROM READERS OF MILLIE'S PREVIOUS NOVELS:

BEYOND THE RED GATE
THE MILLINER
THE NEWCOMER

"I like the way you get right into the story."

"What I like is that there is romance but it isn't smutty."

"Just finished The Milliner and loved, loved, loved it!"

"What a good read, I couldn't put it down."

"My biggest disappointment was that there wasn't a fourth book."

"You kept me up until three in the morning."

"You do have a way with words."

"It should be a New York Times bestseller."

Novels available at: www.amazon.com and www.barnesandnoble.com

About the Author:

Millie Curtis, a native of Oneida, NY, lives on two acres in the County of Clarke, Virginia with her husband of fifty-five years, two dogs and a cat. The distant train whistle echoes, the Blue Ridge Mountains smile and the farmer goes about his daily tasks. It's a peaceful existence sandwiched between the hub-bub of the Washington area and the changing scene to the west. The kids are grown, the grandkids are great, and retirement is a welcome reward.

CPSIA information can be obtained at www.ICGtesting.com
Printed in the USA
BVOW08s0010111016

464704BV00001B/3/P

9 781612 862323